NORTH FORK

NORTH FORK

Wayne M. Johnston

Black Heron Press
Post Office Box 13396
Mill Creek, Washington 98082
www.blackheronpress.com

North Fork is a work of fiction. All characters that appear in this book are products of the author's imagination. Any resemblance to persons, living or dead, is entirely coincidental.

ISBN (print): 978-1-936364-20-6
ISBN (ebook): 978-1-936364-21-3

Black Heron Press
Post Office Box 13396
Mill Creek, Washington 98082
www.blackheronpress.com

For Sally

Corey

It was a bad day from the start. But by midnight, I had cooled down quite a bit from the way I felt in the afternoon when I wanted to kill Harold. Harold's my stepdad. It was his first day home from work, and of course we got into it. Harold Hopp. He never adopted my older sister and me. It's the one good thing my real dad, who's not mean or anything, but is an alcoholic and otherwise pretty useless, did right. He stopped the adoption, so only my mom and Tristan are Hopps.

Harold works on a tugboat out of Seattle, moving oil barges around, and is gone a lot, but it's unpredictable. Sometimes he's just gone overnight and sometimes it can last a week or two, but you never know when he'll show up, so it's hard to relax when he's gone. He's the captain, and when he shows up, he thinks he has to whip me back into shape. At midnight, I was walking on the road that runs across the flats toward town from the gas station at the highway; I should have been somewhere, anywhere, else.

My grades are bad because I'm a procrastinator and some of the teachers are jerks. If I don't like a person, it makes the class suck, and I can't focus even when I know it might be kind of interesting if I did. I've been cutting class some too because the weather is nice, and that would have been enough for him, but what pushed it over the edge was the suspension notice from the principal who now thinks I'm a Nazi skinhead wannabe or something. What's crazy is I don't think I'm racist at all. Racists are everywhere and no one does anything about them. I hate them.

I moved here when I was in middle school. No one would know it because I'm not dark, but my mom is part Native. She's darker than I am, but so are a lot of white people. She was adopted and I've never met any of her real family. She downplays that part of her heritage and I only know about it because it slipped out once when I happened to be paying attention. It's never been something I gave a lot of thought to until coming here and being around all the reservation Natives. I still don't think about it much. It's not like being part Native can fix my life or anything.

We were just goofing around, this kid from the rez and me. He's kind of a loner too. To him this valley is like Israel and Palestine are to Jews and Arabs. It belongs to his people and he thinks it's been stolen. Anyway, that day we weren't thinking, just goofing around. We read *The Diary of Anne Frank* freshman year and then I read a lot more about the Nazis and how they killed a lot of innocent Jews. But at that moment, the Nazi stuff seemed like ancient history, far away and not very real, and we weren't expecting anyone to be paying attention when we did the *seig heil* thing, raising our arms as we passed in the hall. Boy, were we wrong. Two teachers saw us and the next thing I knew, I was being herded to the principal's office.

Actually, I don't think he's a bad guy, the principal, Koenings. He's not naturally mean like Harold Hopp, but I can't talk to him. That tight thing that happens around my heart always comes when I'm around him, and I choke up and can't talk straight. I piss Koenings off. We have history. I get in a lot of stupid trouble over little things. He says I'm wasting my abilities because I'm smart enough to be a good student and am blowing it off. He's given me a lot of chances, but it's not like I can just become someone else and have this different life because he thinks it would be good for me.

The *seig heil* thing really pushed his button. I've seen plenty of rage before, and he was there already when I walked into his office, so of course it sets me off too, and I defend myself because I know I'm innocent. I'm obviously not a Nazi, and I'm no more racist than he is. We were being ironic, and if they had let it stay between the other kid and me, there would have been no harm done, but I couldn't explain any of that because he started out yelling. So I yelled back and included some choice words which made his eyes look like Harold Hopp's, and he suspended me for three days instead of hitting me.

I had a day to myself before Harold Hopp showed up. I just lay around watching TV and reading. Reading is okay if the book's any good. It can be like a movie, only better, because you get to see inside people's heads. I like stories about screwed-up people. Since I'm already depressed a lot, you'd think it wouldn't work that way, but it does. So Thursday I read part of this book about a guy who got his balls blown off in a war, I'm not sure which one. But he and this nympho were in love, only it didn't work because of the missing balls, so he spent all his time drinking while she was running around with other guys. It was a depressing story but it made me feel better about my own life because it showed me that I'm not the only one whose life sucks. I get credit in English class for reading it, and I got the book from the school library.

Harold must have gotten off work at midnight—that's when the boat shift ends, noon or midnight—then come home in the wee hours. He must have needed sleep too, because the explosion didn't come until morning, past the time when I should have been up for school. He had read the mail and was already steaming when he came into my room. I do have my own room. I was sleeping hard and didn't hear him coming up the stairs, but I heard the door crash open, then he had my tee shirt in his fist and was dragging me out of bed.

Compared to me, he's a big son of a bitch, kind of heavy-set and pretty strong. So there he is, in my face with his turtle breath, grey stubble inches away, screaming about what a useless little shit I am (Sorry about the word, but that's what he said). The hypocritical bastard went off about the Nazi salute and how I should know better than to do that crap at school. He's Norwegian or Swedish or something. At least that's what he says, which makes him a squarehead. I don't know where the name Hopp comes from. He's a total racist. When he's not around people who intimidate him, he calls Asians ornamentals, Natives Siwashes and African Americans niggers. You can probably imagine what he calls Hispanics.

He didn't hit me. He quit doing that, thanks to my older sister. She's a year and a half older than me and should be graduating this year, but when she turned eighteen a couple of months ago, she moved out to live with her boyfriend in Seattle. When she was seventeen, she ran away. They picked her up in Portland and she told the cops what it was like around here. CPS came and asked a lot of questions. They didn't do anything to Harold, but he's cautious now. He didn't even slam me against the wall, which he doesn't think of as abuse, and at the perfect slam moment, I could see him stop himself and let go of my shirt, but he made up for it with a lot of words that I'm sure he'd never say in front of someone like Koenings. So after I mowed the lawn and did some other crap that he ordered me to do, he said he was going to Bellingham and left.

I was supposed to study for the rest of the afternoon, and I did read for a while but couldn't concentrate, so I took the SKAT bus into Burlington where I wandered around the Cascade Mall. Mount Vernon and Burlington used to be two towns about five miles apart near the freeway that connects Seattle and Vancouver, Canada. They're pretty much connected now by stores like Home Depot, Wal-Mart, Costco, Best Buy and a lot of outlet malls and car lots and fast food joints. They've pretty much merged into one big sprawl. I met some guys I know at the mall and we got some burgers and went to a house in Mount Vernon on the hill near the high school and the hospital. That kid's parents weren't home, so we hung out at his house watching TV and listening to music.

Someone had some bud, and I smoked a little to make Harold fade, and then those guys decided to go back to the mall to watch a kung-fu movie. Bor-ring! There was this movie I wanted to see playing at the Lincoln, which is a restored vaudeville theater in the old part of Mount Vernon that shows offbeat movies that don't draw a big enough audience for the mall theaters. I made up a lie that I was supposed to meet a girl there and had them drop me close enough to walk. Who knows, maybe if I had stayed with them and gone back to the mall, things might have ended up different. I might not have been on that road at midnight and might not be in this mess now.

Natalie

It was after two when Brad dropped me off, more like three. My aunt doesn't wait up or anything, so I didn't think it mattered. Brad was sort of amazed at where I live, but seemed okay with it. When I got in the house, I could hear Aunt Trish getting up, which was pretty unusual and made me wonder right away what was up. In the little hallway to the bedrooms in her nightgown, half asleep, she looked irritated, like she'd been lying there trying to stay awake, waiting for me. It made her seem old.

"Where's Kristen?"

"She always has to be home by midnight," I said.

"Well, she's not there and her parents are really pissed. They've called about every hour, even though I told them I'd have you call when you got home. You'd better talk to them."

It took me a while to answer.

"What do I say to them? I don't know where she is. I haven't seen her since before midnight."

"You'd better tell them what you know. They were ready to call the police an hour ago. They've probably already done it."

I needed to think fast. Kristen's parents are really anal, very narrow and strict. Certain realities even about Kristen's careful life tend to make them go off and get all hysterical. Kristen's friendship with me scares them and they wish we didn't hang out, but they're nice enough to me. I know it's insincere, and that I needed to be careful what I said, because before she dropped me off Kristen and I were at a party over by Skyline in Anacortes, but her parents thought she was at a movie at the mall.

Sterling answered. He's not even her real dad. She doesn't remember her real dad. Actually Sterling is her second stepdad. She says she has vague, foggy memories of her first stepdad, but the guy on the other end of the phone line has been around for a long time and she goes by his last name and thinks of him as her dad. He's this business guy, real estate or something, pushy in this fake polite way. Right off, he tells me he's called nearly every other kid in the Valley and he knows about the party, so I don't have to lie about that. Everyone says the last person they saw her with was me. It's clear he assumes I'll lie and he's right, I would to help Kristen. He says now he's really worried and just wants to know she's safe. I can tell that at least some of what he's feeling is genuine concern, so I tell him about her dropping me off at the gas station, and I fib a little by saying I knew Brad already and that we'd talked on our cells, and since he was heading home from Bellingham, he'd decided to swing by and take me out to Denny's for a snack where we could talk for a while. Since it turned out good, there's no point in anyone knowing what really happened.

He asks if she said anything about where she was going, so I thought hard and realized she hadn't said much at all, that she had hardly said a word between the party and the gas station. She never actually said she was going home. I was on the phone and just assumed she was pissed about her curfew, and a little jealous that I didn't have one. I was trying to avoid stepping in a milkshake puddle when I got out of the car. Then she drove off. Kristen always has to go home before I do. I didn't even wave or look up. I didn't think I needed to, because we would talk again Saturday afternoon, after the nap I always take when I get home from work on weekend days following late nights.

When I was in middle school, Aunt Trish tried setting curfews and doing the parent thing, but I pretty much did what I wanted and she got tired of fighting it. There was this incident at the beginning of my freshman year, and we had this big blowout and she told me it was up to me to figure it out and I could ruin my life if I wanted. She couldn't stop me. She said I should know from my mom and a lot of other people we know what happens when you drink too much or get caught up with drugs, so she wasn't too worried about that, but I'd better not come home pregnant because she was already stretched thin, just getting by and helping me.

She says she loves me and I believe her. It's not the kind of love you fantasize about from parents, the kind I've hated my mom for not giving me, but it's something. Aunt Trish's got my back. She couldn't have any kids of her own. She had a hysterectomy when she was pretty young because they said she was getting ovarian cancer. In some ways we're like sisters, only she's a lot older. She just doesn't have the resources. She's having a rough life herself. Like the car, for example. I think she'd let me use it, but it's all she's got. She needs it to get to work and if something happened to it, we'd both be screwed. I mean she doesn't even have insurance, so if she got a ticket, it would be a disaster. We live on the rez in an old HUD house but we're not Native. They just keep letting us live here for cheap rent even though my uncle, who is Native, hasn't stayed here for a long time. The house is in his name and I guess, legally, they're still married.

So I didn't get to tell Kristen about Brad–that's his name, Bradley Morgan Stanfield the third, Mister Mercer Island–and the scare he gave me out there by that ditch and that barren field. My night had turned out okay, and I was looking forward to her reaction. I kind of assumed her night would end well too, and she would have a story to tell me. Kristen likes hearing my stories. That's probably why we're friends; our lives are so different. I think it's cool how she asks a lot of questions and wants to hear every detail about some of the dumb-ass stuff my relatives pull. She seems amazed, like I'm living this exotic life, so sometimes I play the story for its effect.

Her life seems exotic to me. I mean she lives in this cool house. It's huge and has a view of the bay. She has her own computer and a TV in her perfect girly room. They gave her a car when she first got her license. True, it was her mom's old Taurus, red, not the perfect color, but it's not that old, maybe five years, and it has a CD player and still smells new.

Brad and I stopped at a restaurant to talk more on the way home. That's why I was so late. He's really a pretty nice guy for a rich kid, and he'd had a rotten day. We probably won't become a thing or start going out, but we got to know each other a little.

I didn't sleep that night, and I don't think Aunt Trish did either. In the morning, I went to work dog-tired, wondering if Kristen had come home and where she had gone. This was really unlike her, so I was a little worried; I was worried even before I called Sterling, but I hadn't let it sink in. I thought about what had happened with Brad and how scared I was, and it made it easy to imagine disaster. I knew Sterling wouldn't think to call me, especially if she was okay, because to him my worry didn't count, and he probably thought I was in on whatever she was up to, so I would have to wait for her to get access to a phone which might take days, considering how much trouble she would be in. I assumed Monday at school would be our first chance to talk. I only wish.

Kristen

I always did the homework. I'm pretty anal that way. That's what Natalie called it. She was always real, nothing fake about her at all. I was just getting to know Corey, just starting to crack open the "valves of my attention," and the connection didn't have time to develop. The valve image makes me picture myself, or at least my soul, which is the essence of me, alone in this cement box like a big bathtub or a tomb, all cold, damp and drippy with a bunch of faucets on the ends of rusty pipes sticking through the walls. If you open most of them, the water that comes out will be freezing and make you so cold you want to die, but there's the possibility of warmth, so that miserable as you are in a dirty, concrete box, you have to try to make yourself feel better. I got warm water from Natalie's faucet. I got a little from Corey that was warm too, or I would have stayed away from him. But it wasn't enough.

You know how sometimes when you read, an idea just jumps out at you and you know it's true, or at least you recognize it as important even if it doesn't make complete sense at the moment, and it sticks with you? It isn't always reading that does it. It can be a song you hear, or a poem, or even just something in a magazine, but sometimes there will be these words, usually just a few lines that stick in your head. Well, it happened to me in English class not long after Christmas break, and it started this thing going that I couldn't let go of. It became the obsession that landed me here. I must not have wanted it to stop or I would have ended it. But I didn't.

It was a normal English class morning, nothing unusual

until it hit me. We had been reading poems that week by Emily Dickinson whom everyone thought was weird because she was a pretty alone kind of person. She wrote this one poem about the soul selecting its own society—choosing only one other soul to let in, then shutting everyone else out, shutting the "valves of her attention." She was interesting because she kept writing even though she didn't get money for it or become famous, and her poems got me thinking, but it wasn't just Emily's words that set me in motion. There was also this guy named Walt Whitman, and some other things that happened.

Whitman's poem was called "There was a Child Went Forth," and I had read it the night before even though I know half the people in the class don't do the reading, but it was assigned, so I had to. Smith asked a few questions about it just to see how much of it we got, and I have to admit, it pretty much went right past me. It seemed like a meaningless string of words, and when I got to the end I was clueless, so when Smith asked if anyone wanted to try and explain it, I didn't raise my hand.

He read it once through, and it really helped to hear it. I started to see images of this kid learning more about the world, experiencing farm animals, water, mean kids, drunks. Then there were these lines:

Affection that will not be gainsaid, the sense of what is
  real, the thought if after all it should prove unreal,
The doubts of day-time and the doubts of night-time, the curious whither
  and how
Whether that which appears so is so, or is it all flashes and specks?

It's about how you question reality. How sometimes you wonder if anything is real. It wasn't like this was a new idea to me, but I think it made me realize just how much I felt that way, like I was dreaming my life and none of it was really happening.

Hearing Smith read it out of a textbook right there in school, written more than a hundred years ago by this famous guy, freed me to let the feeling come to the front of my head. It made me understand a little better about gay people, and how living your whole life pretending to be different from what you are makes you crazy, and if you don't get too depressed and do something fatal, eventually you might get brave enough just to be yourself.

That's what happened to me. I'm not gay, but I've been faking my life big time. That passage in that poem made me realize that the reason I felt so bad was that my life was mostly a big lie, and it had became too difficult to live it, even though it was all I knew how to do, all I'd ever done. After that morning, it kept getting harder to go through the motions.

Natalie

That little weasel! Corey! Goddamn him! The image I get in my head of him doing that to Kristen makes me want to throw up. Jesus! I know he did it. When she started talking to him at school, I knew he would be trouble, but not like this. Shit! Shit! Shit!

The cops were waiting at my house when I got home from work Saturday afternoon. They still acted pretty clueless, like they didn't know yet what really happened to Kristen even though Corey was already in jail, and they came on to me like they thought she ran away or something. Since I was the last to see her, they grilled me pretty hard. The cops pretend to be nice, but it's fake. They're trying to trap you in a lie and you'd better have your story straight. I had to tell them about going with Brad, but I left out a lot, and I had to give them his cell number because I told Kristen's stepdad I had it and that we were old friends and of course he'd passed every detail on to them. I knew they would grill Brad too, so I had to call and fill him in (which he was cool about, considering how stressful the day we met had already been for him) before they surprised him with a lot of questions.

While the cops were still talking with me, one of them got a call about Kristen's car being found in the parking lot at the mall near the theaters. They were pretty tight-lipped, which is their job, I guess, and I think they only let me know about the car to see if it would make me open up and say something I was holding back.

Jesus, if I knew, I would tell them. I was worried sick. I'm still sick only it's gone beyond worry. Then I just wanted to know where she was, probably a lot more than they did. I hadn't let myself imagine the worst yet, at least not in a way that stuck. Now I have this awful feeling because I can imagine Corey doing it, I mean all of it, hurting her, killing her and everything, and I can't shake the pictures in my head of her body all pale and waxy-dead, buried like you see in the movies, in some shallow grave in the woods or tied to a weight at the bottom of the river or out in the bay. He had her car, so her body could be anywhere.

I don't know what she saw in him. He's a goddamn weasel loser. I've seen him be nice like you'd almost believe it, and he's smart enough to be dangerous. The core is rotten. He's an asshole and I'll never forgive him. When Kristen started talking to him I warned her about him, but I didn't tell her why I hate him, because I didn't want to talk about it.

"Trust me, Natalie," she said, "He's not that bad. You usually don't judge people."

It's true, people misjudge me, so I try to be fair. Kristen didn't judge me. That's why we're friends, but her parents still do—judge me, I mean. Usually I can win people over if I want to bad enough. I've made mistakes too, but I really did learn from them, and changed. I didn't tell Kristen why I hate him, because I really am ashamed and I don't like to remember. She didn't live around here then. I'm sure she's heard about it by now anyway. There aren't any secrets around this place. Maybe she didn't hear until after she got to know me. She never brought it up, so I never said anything. But he was part of it, and I can't forgive him.

Okay, so remember how I said there was this incident and Aunt Trish and I had a big blowout about it? The blowout itself didn't straighten me out. It was the incident, and it's really embarrassing to talk about, but it made me think a lot, and it involves Corey, so I'll tell you, but I won't get graphic or anything.

I developed kind of young and the older boys started paying

attention to me even before I was in high school. Since I was sort of unsupervised and pretty much on my own, I went to parties and there was this guy who's graduated now, but he was one of the cool juniors at the time, and I had a crush on him. Because of my mom, I've had to think about drinking a lot, and now I don't do it much, but back then I was still testing it out, and sometimes I thought that because my mom is the way she is, I was just doomed to becoming like her, and anyway I was drinking that night at this party. I was a freshman and this guy who I thought was way cool was feeding me hard lemonade and treating me like I was special and like he really liked me, and we ended up in one of the bedrooms, and that goddamn Corey was in the closet with a video camera. I found out later it was all a set-up, that they had made a bet on it.

What happened was awful enough, but what saved me from something that could have been a whole lot worse was that I wasn't completely blotto, and Corey had drunk enough to be unsteady. While I was getting myself back together afterwards, I heard this noise from the closet like someone's in there, and the door, which was cracked, came open more, so I looked inside, and there's Corey, camera in hand. I went fucking ballistic. I mean I completely lost it. I started screaming at Corey, expecting the asshole I'd been on the bed with to join in and beat the shit out of him or something. I didn't know the whole sorry story yet.

I used every swear word I've ever heard. It wasn't pretty, but it wasn't nearly enough. I grabbed the camera and threw it at Corey. He ducked and it missed and bounced off the doorjamb, then fell to the floor, broken with the tape holder popped open. I had the presence of mind to take the tape out and stomp on it and I kept screaming at Corey and tried to kick him in the balls, and the bastard who fucked me was just sitting on the bed trying to act all innocent, but he couldn't keep himself from laughing, so I screamed at him too and threw the ruined camera at him, then broke down crying and picked up the smashed tape and left.

It was a pretty traumatic experience and it changed me. The sex wasn't my first time or anything, so that wasn't the main part of the trauma. I'd walked in on my mom a couple of times when I was little and Trish has guys over sometimes, so it's not like I think sex has this giant significance. And it didn't make me hate guys in general or anything like that. I got suckered bad, and I hated the people who did it, but only them.

The traumatic part was the way I felt used and humiliated, fucking lied to. I mean I felt small and hurt and pissed-off, and I decided I never wanted to feel that way again. When she calmed down after the big fight we had, Aunt Trish was great about it. She let me talk it all out and helped me get over feeling like a slut, like she really understood because she'd had something humiliating happen to her too, only she never came out and told me any details. She helped me try to figure out what to do to move on. That was when I started to believe she loves me. It did change the way I look at sex, and I don't sleep around anymore. In fact, I haven't done it since then, but that doesn't mean I wouldn't if the right situation came up and I trusted the guy.

Anyway, that's why I already hated Corey and thought he was a slime-ball before any of this happened. And maybe he didn't kill Kristen, and I hope he didn't because I miss her and don't want her to be dead, though it's hard to believe she's not since I think he's capable of it and things rarely turn out better than they seem. After all, this is the land of serial sex killers, like Ted Bundy and Gary Ridgeway. I know she always stopped and gave him a ride when she saw him on the road, even late at night. She wouldn't have hesitated to go out there. I know she walked up Sugarloaf Mountain with him, but at least that was in the daytime, and a lot of people go there, so he probably thought it was too risky to do it then. It's just plain creepy that he had all that stuff by the river and would slink around out there alone in the night, plotting.

Corey

She had this perfect image. I just realized they've got me doing it, talking about Kristen in the past tense, as though it's true that she's gone. And it's confusing because more than anything, I want her to be alive. The odds are always against what you really want happening, so I find it easier to believe bad stuff. But it makes me feel like I've betrayed her somehow.

She *has* this perfect image. She's way too perfect for me, and I couldn't believe it when she started talking to me in English class. I mean none of those girls ever talk to me. It's like I've got loser stamped on my forehead. It's not that I'm ugly or anything, or at least I don't think I am, though I'm really short, but they avoid me like poison and when I ended up sitting behind her, I expected her to ignore me, and she did at first.

She's tall, at least compared to me. It made it strange when she started waiting for me and walking out of class with me. I feel funny about being short anyway, but walking next to her and being eye level with her shoulder and her being so damn perfect and beautiful made me really want to disappear, but she was too nice. I mean she made me feel like what I said meant something and I was worth something, so I had to act like I was.

It was Smith who got it started. He's our English teacher and he makes us write stuff in a notebook all the time. Besides what we write in class, over the year, we have to write an eighty-page journal about our lives, about the people, places or events that made us who we are. That's part of why I'm writing this; at least that's where I got the idea. We can write it any way we want, and I hope Smith will read it, even though passing English seems pretty pointless now, but I'm writing it like a memoir to tell my side of the story in case it matters to anyone.

In class Smith makes us write our thoughts about some idea or question he puts on the board, always heavy, like you would actually want to think about that stuff when you're still trying to wake up. There's five or six people, girls and guys, who sit to the right of me. They straggle in late, smelling of pot, and when I'm thinking about what to write I imagine being one of them, trying to sort through and find words to make sense out of a statement like, "Freedom's just another word for nothing left to lose." I couldn't even start.

This one was about truth. "How do you determine truth?" It had a connection to what we were studying that I could sort of see. Smith said the guys we were reading in our textbook were a bunch of outlaws who wanted to overthrow the king. They thought they were right and the king was wrong and the stuff they wrote was them trying to prove that the way they saw the world was the truth. Kind of like me now. I don't want to overthrow the king, just my stepdad, and I sure seem to live in a different reality than the one the cops live in.

Until now, I wouldn't have tried very hard to persuade anyone that I was more right than they are because I hate having someone else's bull stuffed down my throat. I just want to be left alone, only now they think I killed her, and when I pull back and look, it doesn't surprise me a whole lot. When I was with her I didn't feel much need to prove anything, but now I sure as hell need someone to see things my way.

So that morning, the morning I learned she knew I existed, I'm sitting behind her. I haven't talked to her at all, and to me she's Miss Perfect with this squeaky clean, 4.0 GPA life, and I can see over her shoulder that she's got nearly a full page before I get anything down. Her clean, girly, lotion smell mixed with the pot smell from the stoners is distracting, and even though I hadn't smoked anything, I can't think of what to say. When she started on the second page, I had to do something. Here's what I wrote:

"What is truth? Most of the time life feels like a bad dream that I can't wake up from. Is that reality, or is Kristen's perfect life more real? I suppose what we all do is let our experience guide us. That Patrick guy in the book said that's what he did. Hell, I don't even know if this desk is real or if this assignment is all a dream. Are you real, Mr. Smith, or did I make you up? Was it real when I was a kid and my dad would come home drunk and my mom would scream at him? When I was ten and she took us camping at Deception Pass and I got up to pee and she was moaning in the tent at the next campsite with the asshole who is now my stepdad, was that real? How do we know what's true? You tell me."

We don't have to hand in our notebook right away, and we can put the stuff we write in class in a special section in our journal. Mr. Smith collects them about once a month. I wonder if he actually reads them. After we write for five or ten minutes, he sits up there on that stool and makes us talk about it. Kristen nearly always has something to say.

"It's like the scientific method," she said. "You form a hypothesis, then you test it, and if it works, it becomes a theory. If the theory holds and can't be proven wrong, it becomes a law, like gravity."

"What's a hypothesis?" Smith always makes us define the words. He'll make someone tell him what a theory is and what a law is. Before the "Give me liberty or give me death" guys, we read this play about the Salem witch trials where they hung a bunch of people and a couple of dogs because some girls lied about dancing in the woods, which was against the rules. People were greedy and had things to hide and they believed in the devil and that if you signed his book you could send your spirit out to hurt people. Smith brings up the trials.

"What was missing in the witch trials?" This was a test question. He calls on one of the stoners and actually gets the answer.

"Evidence."

"What's evidence?"

He calls on me even though I don't have my hand up. I say, "Proof."

"Explain what you mean."

"You know, proof, facts, something you experience. Witnesses, maybe"

"In the play, Goody Putnam experiences the death of her babies, and the court experiences the girls bearing witness to Mary Warren's spirit tormenting them in the form of a yellow bird. Did that prove the accused were witches? Are there witches? Was there a yellow bird? How could you prove your answer? The play was about people who had real lives and they experienced being hanged by their government for the crime of witchcraft. Does that make witches real?"

Kristen says, "They were superstitious and scared."

"Would they have agreed with that? What causes people— you, for example—to make the leap into accepting something as truth?"

"You have to be able to test it," Kristen says.

Smith comes back with, "What about things you can't test for yourself? Do we have to test everything?"

"You just go with the way you've been brought up." This comes from a girl in the front row, a cheerleader who gets good grades and is on the ASB with Kristen.

"Do me a favor, Leslie," says Smith. "Go back by the door and flip that little plastic switch."

She does it. The lights go out and the room is dark except for the light coming through the Venetian blinds that cover the single window.

Smith: "What just happened?"

Someone says, "She turned off the lights." The stoners think that's funny and laugh.

Smith: "So what made the lights go out?"

Someone from the class: "She flipped the switch."

Smith: "True, but what really happened?"

Me: "Moving the switch opened the circuit, cutting off the flow of electricity to the lights."

Smith: "Are you sure? She might be a witch who just sent her spirit into the wall and made it get dark."

I've helped my cousin work on cars enough and paid enough attention in science class to know how an electrical circuit works. In fact, he helped me wire a parallel circuit and a series circuit on a board for the middle school science fair. I say, "It's electrons flowing through a conductor from a generator that excites some gas in those light tubes."

"Prove it. I want evidence. Have you ever seen an electron?"

Jake the farm boy hollers out, "No, but I pissed on an electric fence once, so I believe in them." Everyone laughs.

"Witches!" says Smith. Then he says, "Okay, maybe it's not witches, but the explanation for electricity is not something that you can easily witness. We witness and experience the results. They are predictable and repeatable so we accept the explanation as truth, but each of us didn't have to do all of the experiments, follow all the steps, experience the process. We accept a lot of what we consider truth on faith, out of trust in sources that we consider to be authorities, like teachers, our parents, the government, because it helps make our lives easier, more predictable, and we only raise questions when something goes wrong, like when the government arrests our family members as witches, or taxes us too heavily. Then we have to reevaluate what we consider truth."

"Sounds like devil talk to me." I said it. Smith laughed. The bell rang, and as I put my book in my backpack, I felt her standing over my desk, smelled the hint of strawberries, and about froze when it dawned that she was waiting for me.

Usually when I get that fluttery feeling I do something obnoxious, make some crack, but for some reason I didn't. I just acted like it was perfectly normal for her to be waiting, standing above me all tall and graceful, smooth-skinned and olive dark, thick, full-bodied hair hanging to her shoulders, like she could be part Native or Hispanic. I had been staring at the back of her head for days. She wasn't wearing make-up, didn't need to, no zits at all. And those big brown eyes. That's when I noticed the sadness, or at least that's what I decided it was later. At the time I couldn't have explained it. All I knew was that there was something in her eyes that made it safe for me to act like I expected her to be waiting for me, and it changed the fluttery feeling so that the spinning in my head was a rush, a high that I wanted to hang onto, instead of spinning out of control, running from it.

We started talking after class and once in a while we would walk together in the halls. I don't drive for reasons having to do mainly with money and my stepdad, so I hitch rides a lot, or walk, which sucks when it rains. Sometimes when she was going my way, she would pick me up, and we sort of became friends and started talking about the crap that was happening in our lives. Now they think I'm the witch that made her disappear.

Natalie

I'm the last person to have seen her before that bastard got her. I didn't even say good-bye, so the night she left gets played over and over in my mind. It's the night I met Brad, and it was already quite a night before I got home and learned Kristen was missing. I'll try to tell it the way it felt as it was happening, starting when she dropped me off at the gas station out by the highway.

I start to get out of the car. Josh and Alex aren't far behind us. They'll stop for gas and, if the right attendant is on duty, beer before heading to a party in Bellingham. I talked with them a few minutes ago and said I'd call back if I decide to go. Before my foot hits the ground, I have a near miss with a sticky puddle of chocolate shake. The squashed paper cup warns me in time or I would have messed up my sandals. Kristen has to move the car ahead so I can get out. Then the elevator music hits me. The song blasting through the outside speakers is ancient, about home and love waiting. I'm not ready to go home.

The cashier may be Josh and Alex's guy, and I hand him a twenty. He gives me cigarettes and change. For the moment I'm not broke. I clean toilets and make beds at the Cormorant Inn and the job sucks, but I'd be screwed without it. I focus on putting the money and cigarettes in my purse. The heavy glass door isn't the kind that opens automatically and when I reach where I know the handle should be, my hand is surprised by empty space. I look up and there's this guy in my way. He's wearing a baseball hat backwards. Corny, but he's good-looking. His warm eyes make me forgive the hat and the diamond earring that has to be fake.

He smiles and says,

"Hi."

Just "Hi," but he meets my eyes and there's something about the way he says it, and the smile, that makes me lock in and look deeper than I should. I smile back. He steps aside and holds the door open. I can feel him checking me out as I pass and it doesn't make me feel icky. I catch myself smiling at him again.

Outside, I take out my phone. The battery is friggin dead. A few cars are gassing up, but no one I know. No Josh and Alex. So I stand by the rack of exchange propane bottles and light a cigarette, wishing for my own car, but there's no way cleaning toilets and dumping wastebaskets of empty beer and wine bottles and an occasional used condom will get me a car. Aunt Trish's old Granada is so ugly I don't really care that she won't let me drive it. It's that copper color, all faded now. The color was gross even when the car was new, back in the eighties before I was born. I hope someone I know will show up before he comes out.

The station and nearby restaurant are surrounded by fields. There's nowhere to go to avoid him, except maybe to fake a call at the broken phone booth, and I'm not about to do that. They want to make the station look like a circus or some happy place you'd like to go, but instead it feels sleazy, like a used-car lot in the middle of nowhere. Those stupid, bright plastic pennant things flutter and whip, making it sound windier than it really is. They have them strung up between the roof over the gas pumps and the glaring yellow monster sign you can see from the highway. Sticky tire-tread splotches trail across the grimy asphalt from that milkshake I almost stepped in.

Now he's in front of me grinning, not scary at all, and I'm discovering I'm glad to see him even though I don't think I'm his type; my hair is dyed maroon and my nose and eyebrow are pierced. I do like sports. They didn't have a girls' soccer team my freshman year, so I played on the boys' varsity team and lettered.

That helps me with guys.

"Need a ride?"

I hesitate, then say, "Thanks," and follow him to a new midnight blue Honda with tinted glass and expensive rims that each probably cost more than the Granada is worth. He unlocks my door as he walks around to get in and says,

"Where are you going?"

"Depends."

So now I'm in the car with him and he's on the I-5 southbound ramp heading towards Seattle. He's playing some hip-hop CD I don't know. The backbeat from the subwoofer in the trunk pulses through my seat as he accelerates onto the freeway. It's too early for the road to be deserted and slow drivers occasionally block the fast lane. The way he's weaving around them, finding open road, makes me think he's used to driving fast. It's a nice car, comfortable, low to the ground. I'm liking the way it feels, the sense of openness ahead, and that the Valley will soon be behind me.

As the highway rolls by, he hands me a flat bottle. In the light from an overhead sign, I see the picture and the words "Wild Turkey" on the label. The bottle is new and unopened, so I take off the lid. It smells sour and gross.

"You actually drink this stuff?" I say. "It stinks. Does it taste better than it smells?"

I love parties. I like being around people. They can be funny when they loosen up, but I don't like the taste of any of it, and I hate the feeling of being out of control. I like hanging out with guys as friends. Most of the time they leave me alone. Guys are guys and they're going to try stuff, but unless they're creeps, they back off once they know you mean what you say, and then maybe you can be friends.

"It's an acquired taste," he says.

"So you like it?" I say. "You think it tastes good? Or do you drink it for the buzz?"

So far this guy doesn't seem like a creep, and I think I'm a pretty good judge. I can't wait to tell Kristen about this. She'll envy me. I'm still holding the bottle, waiting for an answer.

"Which is it," I say, "the taste or the buzz?"

"It's supposed to be good sipping whiskey," he says, "but it still tastes like paint thinner to me. It's the buzz."

"So why am I supposed to like it?" I say. "Are you trying to get me drunk?"

He doesn't answer and I watch his face, and it's too dark to tell anything. I still have the cap off. I sniff it again.

He reaches for the bottle and I decide to tease him, moving it away toward my window, out of his reach.

"Give it to me!" he says. His voice is angry and sharp, making me tense up.

"You're driving," I say, and continue to hold the bottle away. Now I'm not sure I want to know what he'll be like with whiskey in him.

"Give it!"

"No." I can hear the hint of fear in my voice. Not a good thing to reveal.

He grabs my wrist, the empty-handed one, gripping it so that it hurts. He's very strong and the creep alarms are going off like crazy in my head. The speedometer says 75. Other cars are on the road, but the fast lane ahead is clear.

"Give it, you slut!"

"I'm not a slut," I scream. "And if you let go of my hand and stop acting like an asshole, I might give it to you."

I expect a backhand across the face. Instead his grip tightens. His eyes are fixed on the road ahead and our speed stays steady. He seems to have pulled into himself, far away. I'm still holding the bottle in my right hand. I'm pretty strong too. The grip stays tight and I think about smashing the full bottle into his face but I imagine the car going out of control and both of us dying in a fiery crash. Even though we might cause other cars to crash too, I'm wondering if it could be better than some of the other possible ways this might end. I'm also having this strange but very real feeling that he's hanging on to my wrist in desperation, to keep from slipping over the edge somewhere inside himself.

"I'm not a slut." I make myself say it evenly. "I want you to know that, in case you're going to kill me, you're not killing a slut."

His grip tightens briefly, then relaxes, and he pulls his hand away and puts it on the steering wheel without looking at me or saying anything. My wrist hurts, but I can't rub it without doing something with the bottle.

"So do you still want it?" I ask.

"What?"

"The bottle," I say. "The Wild Turkey?"

"I'm not going to hurt you."

"That's good to know. I'm not sure I believe you, but it's nice of you to say it."

"I'm sorry," he says. "I'm not some crazy psycho. It's been a bad day. I shouldn't have given you a ride."

"And I shouldn't have come, but here I am."

I put the lid on the pint and hand it back to him.

"A deal's a deal."

He opens it and drinks, and now I'm thinking that I should have kept the bottle. He takes another drink, a long one.

"Well, you're not sipping it. I hope the buzz fixes the day."

"Nothing will fix this day." He takes another long drink.

"So are you going to talk about it? Or are you just going to get drunk and be all quiet and scary, because if you're going to get scary again, I want to go back."

"I don't even know you," he says.

"So pull off at the next exit and take me back, and I'll be out of your life."

He switches lanes and takes another drink as he guides the car onto the Arlington off ramp, but instead of heading over the freeway toward the cluster of restaurants and gas stations to let me out or to head back north, he turns west onto a dark road. I can feel without seeing his face that he's back in that faraway place. We're going too fast to open the door and jump. I'd probably break my leg and when he got to me, he'd be really pissed off.

I've never been on this road before. Outside the beam of the headlights, it's all blackness out there. I'm seeing what looks like the beginnings of cow pastures and empty cornfields at the edge of the light. Then I'm thrown forward into the shoulder strap of my seat belt. He's on the brakes hard and we skid, barely holding the road, as we corner onto what turns out to be a bumpy lane between a plowed-up field and a drainage ditch. It's weird what your mind does, but I find myself wondering if he put the lid back on the bottle, or if whiskey is sloshing out on his pants as we bounce down the lane. He abruptly stops, kills the engine and the lights.

My hands look for the seat belt latch and the door handle. As my eyes adjust, I'm able to make out his silhouette. He's slumping over the steering wheel as though he's forgotten I'm here.

My fingers search for the release on the seat belt. I can't get it to let go. My other hand thinks it's found the door latch and I'm visualizing the process of wriggling free, deciding if now is the moment, when he sighs and says,

"I'm sorry."

"Sorry! You bastard! You're apologizing ahead of time so you won't feel so bad after you've left me in that ditch. You better get started, you son of a bitch, 'cause I'm not helpless and it won't be easy." I'm pulling on what I think is the door handle, but nothing is happening.

"I'm not going to hurt you. I want to talk about it."

"Talk! You brought me here to talk? Jesus fucking Christ! Couldn't we have talked on the way back north, or in a restaurant, or in the gas station parking lot?"

"You're right. I'm a son of a bitch, but I'm not crazy. And I won't hurt you, and I don't know why, but I couldn't say it in any of those places, and I have to say it to someone or I'll explode. It's true. My mother is a bitch. A real goddamn bitch!"

"Okay. So's mine. What's so special about that? She's a drunk too, if you want to know. She couldn't get her act together enough to take care of me when I was a kid. She dumped me with my aunt. So your mom's a bitch. That makes it okay for you to scare the living shit out of me?"

"I walked in on them this morning, her and my wrestling coach on the living room floor, butt naked. All I can see is naked bodies and white carpet, him grunting and her moaning. I'm not psycho and I didn't mean to scare you, but I feel crazy. I don't know what I meant or what I wanted, but I'm not trying to hurt you. I'm sorry. I had to tell someone and I can't tell anyone I know."

"Oh Jesus."

"I wish she was dead."

"You only think so. My dad is dead. You don't want her dead."

"I hate her."

"You can do that. If she was dead, you couldn't even do that anymore. Sometimes I still hate my mom too, but it doesn't do any good. It doesn't help her get her act together."

"I hate the bitch. I hate her for what she's doing to my dad and to me." He takes the bottle from between his legs, opens it, and drinks, then offers it to me. "Want some?"

"I'm all right. It doesn't smell like it tastes good, and I've already got an adrenaline buzz going. Does it disappoint you that I won't get drunk?"

"No. Look, I'm sorry I scared you."

"You said that. Maybe I even believe you. You called me a slut. Did you think that because of the way I look, I'd be easy and you could get even with your mother or something?"

"I'm so messed up I don't know what I thought. I don't think you're a slut."

"It must have crossed your mind or you wouldn't have said it."

"Okay, it crossed my mind that you might be easy and. . . Jesus. I've never picked up a girl before. I'm a guy, and after what I saw this morning. . . I mean I don't know. You looked like you needed a ride. Why did you come?"

"I wasn't going to. I mean I never do that either, take rides from guys I don't know. Then I changed my mind when you didn't try to be all cool, but just asked if I wanted a ride. It was a feeling, like I could trust you, like you would have taken me home if that was what I wanted. I can usually tell when guys are weird. You didn't seem weird. When I saw the car and realized your earring might be real too, I wanted to cut and run, but I didn't. So here I am."

"Want me to take you home?"

"Yeah. I think I'm ready to go home now. Look, I'm sorry about your day. You eventually learn to live with the parent stuff, but it isn't easy."

He starts the engine. The lane is too narrow to turn around and he has to back the car out. He goes much slower than on the way in. As soon as we're pointed in the right direction, even before we're up to speed, headlights appear behind us and come up close on our tail. I turn around to look. He watches the mirror.

"Shit!"

He's right. As we round a bend, I make out the silhouette of a light rack on top of the car behind us.

He drives the few miles to I-5 cautiously, just below the speed limit, with the cop car following close. At the on-ramp, he signals and makes the turn. When the cop cruises past, he breaks the silence.

"If you want, we'll find a place to eat in Mount Vernon. Then I'll take you home."

I reached over and put my hand on his forearm, just for a second, to let him know I was okay with it.

That night, I imagined Kristen at home in her tidy room, probably asleep, surrounded by her stuffed animals. I looked forward to her reaction when I would tell her about my night. Instead, I keep replaying images of her and Corey in the car instead of Brad and me, and of all the things I was afraid of that night actually happening to her.

Corey

Kristen is gone, like she evaporated, which is what I was wishing I could do when I was walking in the dark toward town from the highway, sticking out my thumb whenever a car passed because it's a hell of a long walk, even for me who walks everywhere. Natalie was probably the last person to see her, but they think it was me, and I guess if I was them, I would at least wonder too.

The movie I saw that night was about this kid who was having a tough time because he was depressed and his parents had him seeing a shrink and taking all these drugs. He kept seeing this weird guy with a rabbit-head mask that made him do secret things, and an airplane engine fell on his house, making a direct hit on his bedroom, and it would have killed him but he was sleeping on the golf course because of the rabbit guy and he keeps doing what the rabbit guy says, and there's a girl and love and it gets complicated and tragic and ends up being about time travel, or if one certain thing happened different, the whole chain of events afterward would be different. At least that's what I got from it, and right now I'm trying to figure out which thing I could have changed on Friday so that Kristen would be home and alive and I wouldn't be here.

There was this cool song in the movie, at the end. It's really beautiful, about how the world is a sad, mad place which I think is true, and how the best dreams are about dying, and I couldn't get it out of my head as I walked toward town from the highway near the gas station where Kristen was last seen. I was bracing myself to face Harold and my mom when I got back to the house, and I decided not to go there. I've been doing it for a while, not going home. It's worth it if the weather is nice, and Friday was warm and the sky was clear and the Big Dipper was behind me as I walked along the pavement safe from traffic on the extra-wide lane marked for bikes.

There's this place out on the north fork of the river. I first found out about it when I was nine or ten and went fishing for humpies with a kid from school and his dad and uncle. They said it belonged to a farmer, but since it was on the river side of the dike a long way from the farmhouse, and it got flooded sometimes, no one paid much attention to it. Fishermen used it as a place to stop to build a fire and warm up. I kept some camping gear stashed there, and when I couldn't handle being anywhere else, it was my hideout.

If she's really gone like they say, and someone did hurt her the way they think I did, I know I could kill that person. I wouldn't hesitate, though killing him is probably too kind for someone like that because he must already be so miserable that living is probably its own punishment. At least that's the way it feels to me. Most of the time life sucks.

Okay. I admit I have thoughts about weird stuff. And sometimes when I'm really pissed, I imagine having the balls to do something extreme, maybe strap a bomb to myself like someone in Iraq or Afghanistan. But they're not kidding. They— the cops I mean—think I hurt her or worse, even though they don't know what happened, or even *if* anything happened. They actually think I could have... As if I'd do something like that to her.

I watch the news. Sometimes I even read newspapers. It's not like I thought it up myself. You can't turn on the TV without those guys blaring at you about how a bunch of people got blown up by some fanatic trying to help Allah get even with infidels. What

I think it's really about is just being so totally pissed off that life gets blurry for you and you can't sit still and take it anymore, so you pop.

My life is blurry a lot and I get really pissed off at unfairness and the stupidity of some people, like my asshole stepdad. Talk about someone who. . . It would do him good to know fear. And the principal too. They're both full of bull. You'll notice I didn't use the word "shit" here. I would have—I use profanity a lot—but I don't want to put you off, and that word bothers some people. Plus, it doesn't really make my story more accurate, and accuracy is important to me, like when I called my stepdad an asshole. I know that word bothers people too, but it's accurate. He really is one.

Anyway, when they are yelling at me, most of the time I probably deserve it, but it makes my head spin. I get this clutchy, tight feeling around my heart and just want to fade out, become invisible, disappear, but I can't and I have to stand or sit there pretending to listen, so I imagine things, like what if I had a bomb strapped under my clothes like those Arab guys who probably feel the same way. What if I could yell back, or better yet, just open my coat or shirt and watch his (my stepdad's) eyes take it in, and his mouth stop.

I always end it there because if you play it out, it's not so good. I'm not an idiot. I know that bombs kill innocent people, kids like my little half-sister, Tristan. It's on the news every day. I couldn't really do it. I don't believe in an afterlife like the Muslims or Christians. I don't believe in anything, so the only reward would be the immediate result which would include my being vaporized too, and I'm not sure that that's a reward, even though I spend a lot of time wishing I could disappear.

But I could never hurt her. She wasn't having much fun either. It's true—she wasn't, even though she never let on to anyone. On the surface, she seemed to have it all together, perfect grades and everything. The teachers all loved her, but I could sense something about her, like she was scared to let go and breathe. I wish I could talk to her now, but I'm stuck in here and she's gone. They think she's dead and when I let that thought in, let it touch me, certain moments come into my head, and reliving them seems more real than sitting here in this dump. Moments with her, just talking or not talking, maybe just sitting by the river watching stuff float by in the current, or sitting up on Sugarloaf, the Olympic Mountains in the background, with the turkey buzzards from the San Juans soaring above that little lake. I'm discovering, now that I'm locked in this room with nothing to do but think about how she might actually be dead, that it was in those moments that the tight feeling that's always around my heart would relax a little, and I could forget for a second or two that life is a mean joke.

Corey

The room they've got me in is really barren. It's made of cinder blocks and painted pale yellow, which is supposed to be calming or something and is a little better than the usual government-building puke green. But the paint is old and you can tell where people have written on the walls. They've cleaned off the ink, probably with that white-board cleaning stuff I've used to clean the writing off of desks as part of detention at school.

If you look carefully, you can still see the pen-point indentation of letters forming words that, if you wanted to spend the time, you might be able to read. I've got nothing but time here, but I'm not interested in wasting it on that. There's a book we read in Smith's class called Huckleberry Finn with this character, Tom Sawyer, who helps Huck try to free this slave guy. If Tom was here, he would imagine mysterious messages in the writing and be disappointed in me, but I think he was kind of a jerk. I have a hard time thinking of the life of anyone who was also stuck in this room as anything but pathetic.

They're afraid I'll commit suicide, which is kind of weird considering what they think I did. If I was them, I would want the guy who did it to check out. It would save everyone a lot of trouble and money. Of course, as you might imagine from what you know about me, I've thought about it—suicide—and if I was determined enough, which I'm not, I could do it in spite of them, but they have made it hard. There's nothing on the ceiling to hang from except the sprinklers, and if you hung anything heavy from them, it would set off the fire alarm. That would be funny, if you could do it without getting caught, or if it was like the music adding drama to your departure, like on TV, but they'd be in here in seconds to cut you down and then they'd make you feel even more wretched and pitiful than you already feel.

They sure as hell don't want me alive because they love me and would miss me. My life has value to them because they don't know what happened to Kristen and they think I might be able to tell them. They give me books, my schoolwork, paper and a pen to write with, and someone looks in on me from time to time. I'm pretty good at checking out of my body into my imagination, so the slowness of time passing hasn't become excruciating yet, and I want to know what happened to her too.

That night she disappeared, while I was walking toward town and deciding not to go home, they think Kristen picked me up after she dropped Natalie off at the Shell. They think I got her to go to the river with me, which actually did happen, but not that night. They've been to the river and found where I hid my camping stuff and there was some hair that they think matches hers on this fleece I keep there. It does match hers—in fact, it is hers—because she wore the fleece the night she was there. The socks they found are hers too, and so is the blood on them, but there's a good explanation. They just don't believe it.

The night Kristen was driving away from the Shell toward wherever she vanished to, I was walking on the side of the road in the dark, remembering the night the week before when she actually did pick me up. I was dreaming that she was with me again. I know she's too good for me and suspect that, even though she was nice to me, nothing would likely have come of it because if it's good and you want it, it'll never happen, even though there were moments that gave me hope. The dream was nice and helped me avoid thinking about Harold, and it made the long walk out to the trail over the dike go a lot faster.

I quit trying to hitch a ride when I decided not to go into town.

The road out to the dike passes through a lot of farmland, then over a wooded ridge. There isn't much traffic, and on the night Kristen disappeared, only a few cars passed me. Sometimes I play this game with cars, watching and listening for them so I can drop down in the tall grass or find some way to get out of sight before they see me. It only works when there's somewhere beside the road to hide. I started doing it when I was younger and used to sneak out of the house at night. It's still kind of a fun game, and never knowing when Harold or my mom will drive by gives it purpose, but when I hide, I lose the chance that I might get picked up by someone from school and get a ride or have something good happen, like the night Kristen went to the river with me.

The night she disappeared, I was hoping she might show up again, but I knew Harold was still home and I figured he would be really pissed that I skipped out without finishing all his stupid jobs. If he gets mad enough, sometimes he comes looking for me, so I hid from the cars and nobody saw that I was alone. Bad move.

It's a long walk from the highway to the trail on the dike, and when I was hiding from Harold, Kristen couldn't magically appear again like I was fantasizing, but I walk fast and, when it's not raining, I like the night. Even so, I was beat when I got there. The stars were out and there was enough of a moon so that, even without my headlamp, I could follow the narrow trail through the tall grass and low brush that grows on the dike.

I can see pretty well in the dark and it doesn't scare me. Instead, it makes me feel safe, and I like the challenge, but I have this cool quartz headlamp, like a miner's light only better because it's tiny and nearly weightless. It puts out a lot of light, the batteries last a long time, and it's secured to your forehead by an elastic headband. I ordered it from one of those cheap camping gear catalogues, and packed it around with me to use on nights like that one. They have it now as evidence, along with all my other gear from the river.

I didn't need the light that night until it got really dark under the trees that grow between the dike and the river, but then it was safe to use it because you're shielded and can't be seen from any of the farmhouses nearby. I knew if Harold found out about the river place, it would be ruined for me. I held the light in my hand like a flashlight. I know the trail so well I only need to flick it on long enough to orient myself and keep from tripping or running into a tree. When the light is on, I feel like a target because I know how visible it makes me in the night.

You can sense the river nearby like it's alive. You can smell it too, and you're close enough to the bay to get the smell of the salt marsh when the tide is out and the miles of mud flats in Skagit Bay are exposed. The night Kristen was with me, I left the light on the whole time after we got over the dike. It was worth the risk. She walked close to me and held onto my arm, making it hard for me to walk on the narrow trail, so I took hold of her hand and led her. Her hand was warm and trusting. I couldn't have described it like that right then, but it was trust, and it surprised me in the same way I was surprised when she waited after class that first day and talked to me.

That was one surprising night and I hang onto every detail of the memory so I can relive it in my mind. Just like on the night she disappeared, I was walking along the Valley Road, which is the shortest way and the way I always go. It's good that it has very little traffic because the shoulders are so narrow it can be hard to get out of the way when cars go by. A set of headlights passed going the opposite direction, and I didn't pay much attention, looking away to avoid the glare. Then a few minutes later a car came up from behind and slowed to walking speed beside me. It kind of spooked me, and I expected it to be Harold or my mom, even though that night I thought Harold was on the boat, which is why I wasn't hiding from cars.

It can get lonely walking late at night, and I go off into my head fantasizing about things a lot. I was having a lot of imaginary conversations with Kristen in my head, sort of practicing, hoping I could keep from driving her away. Since I'd had a few unspoiled experiences with her, I was thinking we might be developing a friendship or something. Then this car pulls up, and there she is in the shadowy warm glow of dash lights inviting me in. It was kind of like stepping into a spaceship or something from a different dimension. I mean, how often do your dreams come true? At first I couldn't talk, so I felt kind of stupid. It felt unreal, even though I had been in her car before. It smells like vanilla, and though it was a hand-me-down from her mom, it was nice. The high point of our relationship before that night was hiking up this little mountain by Anacortes together. It was a good day. Of course, she drove then too.

When I imagine being with her, my heart gets all thumpity, but for some reason when I'm actually with her, it seems almost normal. So when she asked where I was going that was worth walking that far alone, I told her and showed her where the trail was so she could drop me there. Instead, she pulled the car off the road and switched the engine off. The next thing I knew, we were on the trail in the dark together, and I was floating through what felt like the smoke of a dream connected to substance only by what I now know was the trust that passed from her hand into mine.

The fire pit and the campsite are close to a bend in the river, and when the river isn't threatening its banks, there is a beach with a sand bar. There are no farmhouse lights visible on the opposite side of the river where the high dike rises straight up from the water. The campsite is well protected from view, and even if someone saw the light or the fire, they probably wouldn't think much of it. When the salmon are running, there are many places along the river where people camp. The danger is that someone will think I'm a poacher, or will just get curious, and

Harold will find out. That night I wasn't thinking about that.

I showed her my stash of camping gear that I keep hidden in a hollowed-out place under this big old rotting log that's covered by salal. It even grows out of the top of the log. It's a perfect hiding spot where no one is likely to walk, but even if you went right by it in the day time, unless you were looking for something, you wouldn't see the two plastic five-gallon buckets that have my tent and sleeping bag in them. The buckets are dark blue and used to have Chevron hydraulic oil in them. Harold brings them home from the tugboat. These particular ones still had the lids, so I pried them off and scrubbed the insides with laundry soap. The lids are a little hard to get off, but a screwdriver helps, so I keep a cheap one under the log too. You can put the lids back on easily enough, like on Tupperware. The bad part is if you have to put the stuff away damp, it doesn't dry out and starts to mildew. The gear was all pretty cheap. I bought it on sale at Fred Meyer, so if I had to replace it, it wouldn't be that bad, and like I said, it's all evidence now, so it doesn't matter anyway.

In one bucket I kept the tent and one of those candle-lantern things you can hang from the ceiling, spare candles, some books, waterproof matches and that quick-start stuff to get a fire going when the wood is damp, some packets of instant hot chocolate, a plastic cup, and one of those cheap, aluminum, camp cooking kits. The tent is pretty compact and would sleep two people crammed together. In the other bucket I keep a sleeping bag, a fleece, a windbreaker, and a yellow and black Abercrombie reversible down vest that I traded a kid at school a couple of CD's for. Sometimes I leave some granola bars and Top Ramen noodle packets there too. The bucket lids have kept the mice out.

She thought it was pretty cool that I had it all planned out like that, and that I could go there alone and not feel afraid. I didn't tell her that some nights sitting by the fire or lying in the tent reading, if I let my mind wander I start hearing noises in the brush or maybe just imagining them, and it scares the crap out of me, visualizing all the possible dangers. I even think about sasquatches sometimes. But when that happens, and I think about sneaking out of there and heading back to the house in town, I also think about what it feels like to have Harold in my face or even just to lay in bed in his house, and I decide that the tent isn't so bad and whatever is out there in the dark is just a maybe, while Harold or even the feeling of Harold at the house, is a certainty, so I stay.

When I'm gone all night, I say that I spent the night at someone's house. They used to ask who and I got caught lying a few times, but Harold's gone so much and my mom seems so totally focused on my little half-sister, Tristan, that I hardly exist to her anymore. Even though I was really pissed when I found out Harold got my mom pregnant, you can't hate a baby for very long. Tristan is the only good thing to ever come from that prick, but she makes me feel like a failure even though she's the only person in the world I think might actually love me. I feel responsible for protecting her from the misfortune of having Harold for a dad, which ends up being a bad joke because I can't even protect myself.

I think my mom wishes her life before Harold and Tristan didn't happen, and since I'm part of that life, the wish includes me. Anyway, they don't ask many questions, but when it comes up, I still get yelled at for not telling them where I've been. I would get yelled at no matter what, so it doesn't change what I do. It's better when I don't come home, for everyone.

There was a quarter moon and bright stars that made it nice by the river. You could see the current rippling on the water. Kristen had scratched her leg on some blackberry vines on the trail. She was wearing shorts and running shoes. There was a lot of blood from the scratch, even though it wasn't deep, and it had run down onto her sock. She decided to go wading to clean up her leg and took her socks off. She used the socks to wipe the sand off her feet and then put her shoes back on and left the socks on the ground.

We sat on a log in the dark for a while, watching the river and looking for shooting stars, but we were cold. If I was going to make a move to get her to make out or something, that would have been the time, but I didn't do it. I wanted to. I mean she's beautiful, and there we were in the moonlight, and I could tell she was cold and I wanted to put my arm around her, and, well, you know. . . It makes my head spin, just thinking about it.

Maybe I misread her and maybe she wanted me to at least hold her. Girls can be strange that way, but I'm not very experienced at this stuff. Not like I've never done anything with a girl before, but this is different. It's not just about sex and it's hard to explain, but it has to do with what I felt coming through her hand in the dark on the trail. It's like she sees this part of me that I don't even think exists. She seems to see it the way you see the color of someone's hair or how tall (or short, in my case) they are, and she sort of respects it or is at least interested in it, and because of that I have to start believing in it too, and learning about it, which is really scary.

The only way out would have been to ignore her and stay away, which would have meant saying no to the ride. Or I could have tried to get her to make out or just acted stupid like I usually do, and spoiled it all, driven her away like I do every other good thing. But I kept my hands to myself and offered her the fleece and the windbreaker, now evidence, and asked if she thought we should build a fire.

It was only ten and she said she could stay a little longer if she checked in with her mom on her cell. It was strange but reassuring to hear her lying to her mom on the phone about how she was meeting some of the ASB (student government, I don't even know what the letters stand for) kids at Denny's to talk about a pep assembly. While the fire was heating up, she helped me put up the tent, and then we sat watching the flames and talking.

Actually, now that I think about it, I did most of the talking. And I think about it a lot because, just like the cops, I'm looking for clues, trying to remember if she said anything that night that would help me figure out what happened to her, or if I could have done something different that would have changed the way things are turning out. We talked a little about school. I asked her what it was like to get good grades and have all the teachers like you. She said it was a lot of work and that she had always known it was expected of her, so it didn't seem like there was any other choice. I asked how she got along with her parents.

"All right," she said.

"Do you love them?" I realized as I asked it that it was kind of a weird personal question, but we had been talking about my parents and Harold, so it wasn't completely out of line. Her life seemed so perfect to me, and the lie on the phone surprised me. Going home to people you could tell the truth to and have real conversations with about the stuff that bothered or scared you without them taking it all wrong and going ballistic was one of my fantasies. When my parents were going through the divorce, I used to dream that they would die in a car wreck or a plane crash and I would get adopted by these imaginary people and we would have this happy family. I had imagined her family was like that, and I was starting to sense that maybe it wasn't.

"I don't hate them, not like you and Harold," she said. "We don't talk much. As long as I get good grades and report in so they don't have to worry, they're nice enough. I've never done anything to upset them, except go to a party once in a while. If I keep my grades up, do all the right stuff at school, go to church and say what they want to hear, they leave me alone. He's not my real dad either. In fact he's my second stepdad, but he's nice to my mom and gives her the life she wants. I think they want me to have a good life. I can't wait to go to college and move out. I don't feel like I really know them."

I can't even think about college. It doesn't seem real to me. I'm already short of credits. I couldn't focus on school enough to make it to graduation next year, even before being locked up, so talking about college with her made me nervous. I saw a meteorite streak across the sky and got her to look before it faded, then I changed the subject.

"I just want to leave," I said. "I'd do it now, if I had some money."

"Where would you go?"

"I don't know. Camping on some beach in Mexico sounds good. I hear you can live cheap down there, and it's warm. It would be great except for all the bandit and corrupt-cop stories that make it sound dangerous."

Then I remembered this story my cousin told me about his dad. I told it to her the way I remembered it. I won't tell it here except to say that when my uncle was in high school, he and one of his friends ran away to Hawaii. Eventually they got caught and were brought back, which made Kristen ask,

"So what did they do to him?"

"I don't know the details, only that he became a plumber, which pays pretty well, and married my aunt, and you'd never guess now that he ran away when he was a kid. By the time they caught up with him, they were probably so glad he wasn't dead that they forgave him, like the parents in Romeo and Juliet would have if the stupid kids hadn't killed themselves. All his money was gone. If I had that kind of money, I'd find a way to be gone for good, like my sister. No more Harold Hopp, ever."

She seemed deep in thought, hypnotized by the fire which was dying down, so I threw a little more wood on it and that brought her back. She looked at the time on her phone and said she had to go.

Now this would have been the moment to kiss her, if that

was going to happen. Either then, when we were leaving the campsite, or back at her car to say good-bye, but it didn't happen and what's weird is that even though something about her had changed while I was blabbing away—she was more distant and hardly said anything at all—the trust was still in her hand as I led her along the trail. I don't think I was imagining it, but there was also this sadness. Remember, I had seen it before, only this time it wasn't very well hidden, like if I said the wrong thing she would cry, so I gave her space and didn't try anything.

At the car, she said she had had fun and thanked me for the hot chocolate made out of boiled river water that she drank while I was telling the story about my uncle. Then she was gone, and I went back and sat by the fire alone for a while before climbing into my sleeping bag.

We didn't say much to each other at school the week of the fateful night. She was absent one of those days. Then I got suspended. Friday night, when they think she was with me and I raped and killed her and dumped her body somewhere, was pretty uneventful. It was late and I was really tired when I finally got to the river. It had been a long day. Remember, I had mowed the lawn, hung out at the mall, smoked a little weed and gone to a movie before the long walk out to the campsite. I built a fire and sat by it for a while, thinking about her and remembering. Hidden under the log, I also had a bottle of MacNaughton's that I had boosted from Harold one night when he was too drunk to miss it. There was some left, so I had a few snorts. Actually, it took more than a few to cut the loneliness which was sharper now that she had been there with me, and when I finally got drunk enough to sleep, I crashed. In the morning when I woke up, I was sick and hung over.

Natalie

Okay, so right after the cops were done talking to me that Saturday, the day after Kristen disappeared, I called Brad. I was a little nervous about it. Who wouldn't be? It was a pretty weird night anyway, without adding Kristen to it. But there was no way around it. Brad was involved and when they grilled him, if his story was different from mine, eventually they would trap him into telling the truth. Except for the fact that I let a strange guy who was drinking pick me up, the truth isn't that bad, though it would probably end up including his mom's little indiscretion and would likely start some big Mercer Island high-society scandal. So I thought we could save everyone a lot of trouble and not hurt anything by a little harmless editing to smooth out the wrinkles. Politicians spin the truth all the time. So I called him.

When he answered his cell, he sounded surprised, but seemed glad it was me. It was easy to talk to him. When I told him about Kristen vanishing, he was pretty taken aback, but instead of worrying about how it would affect him, he seemed worried about how I was feeling. Which surprised me. It was nice. I expected him to be mad that he was involved because of me.

We didn't need much of a lie. It was more like we needed to verify with each other what really happened between us, you know, what it meant in the end so it would be clear which details were important to tell and which should be left out. The only part that we had to make up was how we met. The most dramatic and memorable part of the night, the part in the car when I thought he was going to rape me, really was all just miscommunication and my imagination running away. In the big picture it was just a detail, part of our getting to know each other. We decided to say that he just needed to talk about some stuff that was happening in his life, school and ex-girlfriend stuff, and we couldn't decide whether to go down to Everett, which would have been my idea because I wanted to get out of the Valley and I like riding in his car, or go to Denny's in Mount Vernon which would be easier for him because it wouldn't be such a drive to get me home and he wouldn't be out all night.

We figured that the cops who were behind us at the Arlington I-5 exit probably took down his license number, which made it necessary to explain that little side trip. We weren't parked down that lane very long, so we decided to say that on the way to Everett we realized how late it was and pulled in there to talk for a minute and make up our minds what to do next. It really wasn't that long between when we left the Shell and when we got to Denny's since Brad drives fast, and we stayed at Denny's for a long time. The waitresses there can verify that.

The actual lie part, how and where we met, was a little harder. I told Sterling that Brad had called me earlier and we had arranged for him to meet me at the Shell. The cops can check your phone records and since there was no call, we had to figure something out. The Shell is like halfway between Anacortes and I-5, not exactly where you'd choose to buy gas if you just pulled off the freeway. Brad had told me he was heading home after hanging out in Bellingham with some friends who go to Western, but he hadn't explained how he ended up at that particular gas station. It turned out he had just dropped off this kid from Anacortes who needed a ride home. He didn't really know the kid but his Bellingham friends did, and Brad was just being nice. It's comforting to find out that my creep alarm does work, and the reason I let myself get in the car with him is that he really is nice.

We decided that it would be okay if I changed my story

about there being a phone call and admitted that it was a chance meeting, but kept the part about us knowing each other before. If it came up, I would just say that I told it that way to Sterling because he doesn't approve of me and I thought it would sound better if our meeting-up was planned. It turns out that Brad and I know some of the same people and we both go to Bellingham parties enough that it would be safe to say we had met there and knew each other.

If you remember, I was stuck at the gas station because my phone died and Josh and Alex, who were supposed to show up and take me to a party in Bellingham, had gotten another call. They changed their minds about going north and stayed in the Valley at another little gathering, figuring that since I hadn't called them, I must have changed my mind too. When I found myself at the Shell with a dead phone and no ride, and there was my friend Brad, it was perfectly natural to head off into the night with him.

So Brad and I got our story all straight and coordinated, and what was funny was that it was so easy. It felt like we were old friends. There were none of those uncomfortable silences where you know the other person is seeing the situation way different from the way you are and it's hard to decide what to say for fear of being taken all wrong.

What all this means, of course, is that I'm staying in contact with Brad. He didn't just fade back into the night like a dream. He's come up here a few times and we've hung out and we have a great time together. We even hiked up Sugarloaf Mountain together, which is something I wouldn't have done if Brad hadn't been there because Kristen climbed it with that weasel before she went missing. I'm not the granola type. I like being outside and I'm athletic enough and even go running for exercise, but I run on the track at school or beside the road in town, and hiking up some steep, lonely trail in the woods has never been my thing.

Well, after school the day the cops quizzed him—they actually went to his school, which might have been embarrassing for him, but he said he didn't mind—Brad called me to let me know how it went. He said the session with the cops was pretty easy because none of it felt like a lie and the little bit of clarifying we did was harmless and really no one's business but ours. Besides, and he even said this, it feels like we have known each other for a long time. I agree, so when he asked if he could come up on Sunday, there was no hesitation on my part. I just had to think of something to do.

So we hiked up Sugarloaf Mountain. It's not a real mountain, the kind with snow, but Brad says it feels like you could be in the foothills below Mount Baker when you're on the trail. I'd been to the parking lot before, and to the viewpoint on top of Mount Eerie, which is right next to Sugarloaf but has a road to the top and a lot of towers for cell phones and military communications stuff. The view from Mount Eerie is a little better because it's higher. On a clear day, you can see Mount Baker and the Cascades. Looking south you can see the Sound all the way to Everett, and to the west the Strait of Juan de Fuca and the Olympic Mountains, but since you can drive up Mount Eerie, it can get pretty congested and touristy.

We weren't going for the view. Kristen, of course, influenced the choice, and it's true, I thought about her a lot. The trail up is really steep and you don't do much talking unless you stop because the climb takes away your breath. I kept imagining her and that little turd together on the trail and tried to visualize how it was and what they said to each other.

Of course I wouldn't have been there without Brad, and I would have gotten lost without him. He is a hiker and has been all over the Cascades. When I suggested we spend our time together on Sugarloaf, I didn't know he would know what he was doing, and would think to get a trail map from the little kiosk thing by the parking lot, and that we would need it because there are lots of forks in the trail. Even though there were signs with numbers on them nailed to trees, if you weren't paying close attention, even with the map, you would soon find yourself disoriented. Lost.

It's kind of dark in there, like a jungle, all green and brown and damp and cool-feeling. That day, the sunlight hit the bushes, the fallen, rotting trees and the needle-covered ground in yellow dapples. It made me feel good inside even though I felt Kristen's presence. It was a weird feeling because I knew I should be sad for her. And I am, but I wasn't feeling sad at that moment and couldn't make myself feel that way.

Brad kept wanting me to walk ahead because he's a gentleman and it's supposed to be good manners to let the lady walk in front, so he was being nice. But in this book I read for one of my classes written by this Native woman who grew up in eastern Washington during the time the Natives were having to make huge changes to adapt to all the white people who were moving in, she talked about how the early settlers thought it was rude that Native men walked ahead and had the women and children follow. She said there was a good reason, which was that most of their walking was in the woods or in places that belonged to animals like bear and cougars, and the man walked ahead to protect the women and children from attack by an animal.

This was running through my head because last year there were several cougar sightings near town and dogs and cats were disappearing. The paper said that it was probably young cougars and that when they reached a certain age, like teenagers, they had to go out on their own and find their own territory, and since dogs and cats were easy prey, and because there is less and less forest, they sometimes tried places where people lived. There don't seem to be any around this year, but I still couldn't help imagining them lurking in the brush, so I told Brad about the cougar sightings and that I wanted him in front, and that the paper said we should make noise and try to make ourselves seem as big as possible. Of course when he was walking ahead, I couldn't help thinking about what was behind me, but I pushed it out of my head so as not to spoil the day. A little bit of danger's not a bad thing. It can draw people together.

Before you get to the top, there's this nice viewpoint off to the side of the trail with a natural bench formed by an outcropping of black rock that has lichen and moss growing on it. It looks out over the San Juans and the Strait of Juan de Fuca, and is a great place to catch your breath. As usual, Brad was wearing a baseball cap which wasn't backwards this time. He's really a pretty good-looking guy, a little too Abercrombie maybe, but I don't hold that against him. He's pretty normal actually, except for the earring which bothers me only because the diamond is too big and is real.

He has a good build and is in better shape than me. I got him talking about wrestling, which he likes a lot in spite of what happened between the coach and his mom, and he hardly got out of breath at all on the climb. He did most of the talking for the noise to keep the cougars away, and it turns out that he has a real dilemma. He could qualify for the state championship tournament next year with a good chance of winning, so he doesn't want to quit, but he can't imagine working with his coach. It's hard enough being around his mom, even though it sounds like he doesn't see her as much as I would have thought.

His mom hasn't left or anything, but she has an important job and gets home late. They don't eat meals together like you'd expect people to if they could, and since it's not wrestling season, he can avoid the coach most of the time at school. He can't tell how much, if anything, his dad knows. He feels guilty about that. He says his world feels really surreal, like he's living in a different reality from everyone around him, and he wishes his parents would have a big fight and that it would all be out in the open. He knows he should have it out with his mother, but it's like she's dodging him and the more time that passes, the harder it gets and it's almost easier to pretend he didn't see anything, but he did, and it's like the image of what he saw is seared into his brain. So he said he was really glad to see me today because I'm the only one whom he can talk to about any of it.

I was resting next to him at the viewpoint, watching this ship make the turn from the Strait into the passage that leads toward the refineries, and thinking about Kristen and Corey sitting in the same place and about how different they are, or were, from each other, though they both dressed preppy, and wondering what they talked about that day they came up here and what she saw in him that would make her come here with him. The realization that I would probably never get to ask her hit me, and this powerful sadness came over me. Without thinking about it, I put my hand on Brad's and leaned my head on his shoulder, and it felt comfortable, which surprised me and didn't surprise me at the same time.

Then I heard people coming up the trail, kids' voices, a family, and as they got near, I started thinking about how we would look to them, Brad and I sitting there. It made me think about my hair and piercings. I hardly ever think about them anymore because they've become like part of me now.

I could tell, without looking, when the family came out of the woods to a place where they could see us, because the kids' voices changed. They didn't stop talking, but they got quieter, more subdued. They were probably disappointed that we were there, and it was nice that they sensed our moment enough to let us keep it when they could have just as easily barged right up and joined us. It made me think about people and human nature and how Brad and I were both feeling the big sadness, he for his own reason and me for mine, and each reason was because someone else didn't care enough about how what he or she did would make someone else feel.

Our sadness was bringing us together, which was nice and maybe could make it bearable, and this family, even the kids, felt something, though they likely couldn't have said what it was, and without saying anything, pulled back and went on, allowing us to hang on to the feeling a little longer and maybe let the part that was connecting us take root. So for a little longer, we watched the ship, tiny in the distance, make its way north between the islands, and then we followed the trail up to the main viewpoint at the top.

Kristen told me she had seen vultures from up there, which surprised me because I didn't think there were birds like that around here, so I told Brad about them. The family that had passed us wasn't at the top, but there was a couple talking and pointing at landmarks. We looked for the vultures. Kristen said they saw them to the right of Mount Eerie in the distance beyond the little lake that's right at the base of the mountain, and I had this memory from Greek mythology. I do that, as you may have noticed, have memories from things I've read. This one was about birds and came from the Trojan War story, which wasn't about who won the war but about how war sucks and how kings can be wise and good and still lose, or be assholes and win.

Anyway, near the end of the story, the Trojan king, alone except for a servant, is heading across enemy lines to get his son's body back so it can have a proper burial. His wife thinks he's crazy and that he will become a hostage, or be tortured, and will definitely make an already bad situation worse. He says the gods have told him to go and he prayed for a bird of omen, which means a sign from the gods, to show his wife that he's right in going. If the bird comes from the right, it's a good sign, kind of a thumbs-up. If it comes from the left, it's not so good. Where Kristen said she saw the vultures is on the right. An eagle came for the Trojan king. It was on the right and he got to bring his son's body back, but later

Troy was defeated and burned to the ground.

So, were Kristen's vultures a good sign or a bad one? Is she out there alive somewhere, or not?

I told Brad the omen story and we looked for birds. There were some robins flitting around in the brush, but there were several and they were on both sides of us. We didn't see the vultures, and decided they were keeping themselves to San Juan Island, which is where Brad said he had heard they lived. He has a friend whose family has a house there. We heard some crows behind us and turned to look but didn't know if that meant anything, and finally we did see two eagles, but they came over the top of Mount Eerie, so I guess the gods weren't ready to tell us anything. But it was a good day anyway, even with feeling the big sadness, because nothing spoiled the way that sharing it with Brad makes grief bearable.

Corey

It was still pretty early when I woke up. There were a bunch of goddamn crows in a big maple tree above the tent making a huge racket. Their squawking is annoying, like they're always scolding something or bitching about life. My head was throbbing and I had to pee, so I climbed out and watered a bush away from the tent. The leaves were out, it being spring and all. Brightness filtered through to the ground and made blotches on the tree trunks. When I looked up at the crows, who didn't seem a bit afraid of me, the green of the leaves had this yellowness to it from the sun shining through them, and it was a nice morning, in spite of how I felt.

The MacNaughton's bottle had just one good swallow left in it, so I downed it, hoping that it would clear my head. Then I took down the tent and packed the gear back in the buckets. I left everything, including the empty bottle, hidden under the usual log. I have a thing about littering and always carry out in my pack any garbage that won't rot, but since the decision to come was spur-of-the-moment, I didn't have the pack with me.

I nearly made it to town before they picked me up. The sheriff's car came from behind so I didn't hear it until it was close. I looked back and it was clear right away that the cop's attention was focused on me, not on the road or the intersection coming up at the edge of town. He had the radio mike in his hand. Then he put it down and pulled up next to me with the window down.

"Good morning," he said.

I just said "Hi" without looking directly at him. I had whiskey on my breath and didn't want him to smell it. I didn't know what else to say. The last thing I wanted was to get in the car with him, which is what eventually happened. He asked me how I was doing, then started in about what a nice morning it was in that fake polite way public-authority people are supposed to use before they get the Harold look in their eye and grab you or point a gun at you and put the cuffs on. Okay, you should know I've had my run-ins with officers of the law, mostly town cops or Shelter Bay security guys who thought I was suspicious for various reasons at different times. None of it ever came to much. The only thing that stuck was an MIP which means Minor in Possession, and drinking is something everyone does, even cops. In fact, one of the cops that cuffed me got busted later for giving beer to an underage girl who just happened to be sitting in his car up in the park. I wonder what he was after. I had to go to court and pay a fine, but so have half the other people at school. That's a big part of why I can't drive.

It was obvious that something weird was going on, so I'm standing there in the road trying to come up with a strategy, and this other cop car pulls up. The new guys get out of their car. They had pulled off the road in this open area near the sewer treatment plant, and they're standing there with their hands on their guns. The first cop tells me to walk toward them, keeping my hands visible at my sides. By now, it's clear I'm screwed somehow, and I start thinking about how I look, what a mess I am. I'm short, but I've been shaving since I was fifteen and I grow a pretty good crop of stubble over night. I combed my hair by the river but I didn't have a mirror and it gets greasy when I sleep, especially if I've been drinking, which makes me sweat. I'd slept in my clothes. Not a good picture.

As I walk toward the second cop car, my mind is flashing all over the place, looking for options and not finding any. Even though they are acting polite and wording their orders like suggestions, it doesn't take much imagination to see how quick the pretend politeness will disappear and guns will come out if I start running or even just try to ignore them and keep walking. So when they ask if I would mind getting in the car, I cooperate, and when they want to frisk me before I get in, I make a show of assuming the spread-eagle position with my hands on top of the car to let them know I think maybe they're in the wrong movie, and I've got nothing to be afraid of.

They took me straight into Mount Vernon. From the radio talk, I can tell the cop in the other car went by the house and told Harold and my mom where I was, and I was imagining Harold's face at the door and how pissed he'd be. But at the same time he'd be sort of self-satisfied because he thinks I'm scum and this would help him confirm it. I still didn't know what was going on. All they said was that they wanted to ask me some questions. They were still playing the polite game and hadn't cuffed me or told me my rights like they would if they were arresting me.

At the courthouse, which is also the police station, with the big new county jail across the street, they put me in this room like you'd see on a TV cop show where they question suspects. There was nothing there but a video camera mounted in a corner from the ceiling, a crappy-looking table, and some of those plastic chairs like they have in the library at school that are indestructible. The walls were, you guessed it, puke green, and there was the mirror that's really a panel of one-way glass built into the wall.

I needed to take a dump because it was morning and I hadn't yet. I know it's gross and you probably don't want to read about it and I won't go into detail or anything, but I'm including it because it was memorable. They sent a cop with me. Luckily I wasn't cuffed to him, so he didn't have to come into the stall, but he hovered just outside like he was afraid I would escape down the toilet. I could see his feet under the door, which made it hard to go even though I really had to, and that was when it hit me that this was the real thing, and whatever it was they thought I'd done last night, it was a bigger deal than smashing mail boxes in Shelter Bay or even having Sascha Miller sneak out at night back when we were in eighth grade to roll around in a sleeping bag with me. After I made the mistake of bragging it up to some guys at school, she said I tricked her into it and tried to rape her, which wasn't true, but it got all public and I was questioned first by the principal, then by some detective.

It was Sascha's idea to sneak out, and she talked like she'd done it before and seemed to have this big crush on me. I didn't like her all that much, but she wasn't bad-looking. I mean, who doesn't fantasize about doing it? I hadn't done it and it seemed too good to pass up. She even brought a water bottle with some gin in it that she stole from her parents. It tasted awful but we drank it anyway. I probably drank most of it. I stole one of Harold's condoms from the nightstand drawer in their bedroom, but didn't use it because it never got that far. It was close but I stopped, because all of a sudden she tensed up like she had changed her mind, so I didn't go through with it and she was crying and it got real awkward. I'm sure she was lying about having done it, which I understand since it's the kind of lie I would tell and have told, and my mistake was bragging about it, but I sort of got trapped into that.

I did brag. I even said more happened than did. I'm not trying to duck out of that part. But it wasn't the way they tried to make it look, like she was all innocent and I had plotted it out and tricked her. We met in the park and Rebecca Swanson was with her. Rebecca was going out with this guy who has since moved but who met us there too. They went off and left us alone, which at the time I thought was good, but it sure ended up a mess because Rebecca told these two guys who go to our school and who I thought were my friends that Sascha and I had snuck out and were now a couple. They called up all buddy-like and said, "We hear you're going out with Sascha now." I said no, we weren't going out or anything, and they said they heard about last night and how we were in the park together. They acted like they envied me, like I was the luckiest guy in the world and said, "You guys did it, didn't you?"

I didn't deny it. I would have felt stupid saying what really happened and, looking back, I don't think the truth would have helped much anyway because there still would have been a rumor and her parents probably would have heard it and Sascha would likely have made up a similar lie because that's the way she is, so I should have just said nothing happened, but I wanted to be cool and let those guys think we did it and that's part of why I'm still stuck in here. There are a few other messes I've been in that aren't helping much either.

When I got back into that puke-green room with the camera, these two cops came in and made me tell them every little detail about how I spent all the time from when Harold went to Bellingham, leaving me home alone, until the cop spotted me that morning. I've already described that time to you, so I won't bore you by repeating it here. I could tell they knew a lot of it already, at least up until I got dropped off at the Shell a little before midnight. But I didn't want to tell them about the campsite because for some reason I still had this sense that I would get to walk out of here pretty soon, and I wanted to protect that place so that Harold's house wasn't my only option. I ended up telling them, but they had already found out from someone else, so it didn't matter.

As I said before, I have trouble with authority and I get this tight thing in my chest. In fact, I tighten up all over and it gets hard for me to breathe. Whenever I'm put on the spot, my voice cracks, and I probably look all desperate or something, and I sort of am. I can never think straight and I end up doing one of two things. Sometimes I clown, like when they asked if they could frisk me, and sort of make a big show of overdoing whatever it is I have to do. The other thing I do is get angry and belligerent and try to push the situation over the edge and get it done with. When I can make Harold or Koenings lose it, even when I end up getting thrown around or Harold hits me like he used to do, I feel better. When I make them lose it, I feel less crappy, because I know I'm not the only dumb shit in the world.

That day was no different. The tight-chest thing came as soon as the first cop pulled up beside me. As you may recall, I looked like a mess, with face stubble and dirty, slept-in clothes. The clown bit didn't seem to work at all. Those guys had some serious faces that wouldn't crack even the start of a smile, and now that I know what they think I did, I understand, but I didn't know that yet, so I acted pretty unstable. In fact, I was a mess when I got back from the bathroom where I'd realized that this was no game. My mouth was dry and my voice was cracking when I told them about mowing the lawn and reading a book before I headed for the mall.

So I didn't come off as very believable. I mean, looking back over it, since I've got all this contemplation time on my hands, remembering how I said what I said, knowing now what they must have been thinking and how crazy angry I feel towards anyone who might have hurt her when I let myself imagine it, I can understand why they're keeping me here, even though all their evidence is circumstantial. I don't have any way to prove she wasn't there that night. What I told them sounds like a lame story, even to me. I act guilty and look guilty because I'm used to being the one who caused the trouble, and even though I don't have a long police record, in this valley everyone knows everything about you. If you started stacking up the stories about me and believed the worst of them, it wouldn't be hard to believe I did it.

Since I'm only seventeen, they can use the fact that I'm a minor to keep me locked up without charging me. My mom and Harold aren't going to do anything to get me out, and my dad is probably just drinking more, if that's possible. The worst thing is that when they get their case together, they'll probably try me as an adult.

Kristen

Being here has changed me. Now, instead of fighting the urge to run Bonnie's Taurus into a tree, I'm trying to figure out how to stay alive. But I haven't cut myself once since I got here. After you've seriously thought about killing yourself, life starts to seem like a game you can get out of anytime you're brave enough to move the steering wheel half an inch.

"Give me liberty or give me death." Another quote out of a textbook. For me, instead of liberty, it's give me honesty and some kind of warm connection. Until I met Grant and he got weird, I was starting to feel okay about myself, in spite of my fabricated life here. Sometimes jogging, or sitting on the beach, I would realize that what I was feeling at that moment might be happiness.

Now I'm scared. It's a toss-up whether being depressed all the time or being scared is worse. The phone is on the table, and I could pick it up right now and go back to being depressed, but I'm trying to be adult. I could call Natalie. If she felt this way, I would want her to call me. But I can't go back to being Kristen again, and Sterling and Bonnie would never allow me to be anything else.

Grant is scaring the shit out of me. Natalie might know what to do, but I can't make myself call her yet, because I know it would bring this to an end, and bad as it has become, I'm not ready for that.

So I live here day to day, moment to moment.

It started out as a game, coming here. It gave me a kind of hope.

The scheming was fun and a good distraction. I mean plotting my escape, buying the hair coloring, the clothes and make up, pretending to spend money that I was really stashing away in a book in my room. It was like the little-girl fantasy games I used to play with my stuffed animals, and until I ended up across the border here, with no one to recognize me or get in the way, it could have stayed a game.

Natalie is really pretty and has a nice figure, but she covers her looks by dying her hair that maroon color and wearing it short. Sometimes she uses gel to shape it. One night we were messing around at her house with some of that spray dye that you can wash out and I did my hair half her maroon color and half orange, and I put on make-up just to see, and it was truly weird how much the dye and the eyeliner changed my appearance. Looking in the mirror, I imagined what I would look like wearing clothes like Natalie's, my hair dyed a different color and cut short, or even done up with gel. Most of her clothes didn't fit me, but we found an outfit that did. It was startling. I really did look different.

After I cut it, I did my hair, not all of it but enough, this red color. To me it's kind of garish and isn't anyone's natural color, but it's not likely to attract as much attention as maroon. I've gotten used to my new look. I made the changeover in the bathroom at Amanda's cabin. The nearby houses are all summer cabins too, so no one was around to see me. I got in with the key I knew was hidden by the light on the back porch. It felt like I was playing a game.

I've watched enough "Crime Scene Investigation" shows on TV to know that if they really did a search, I was probably leaving all kinds of evidence. But I was as careful as I could be not to leave traces of myself, and I assumed that they wouldn't think to look there. Amanda's in my class at school. Her parents were hippies when they were younger and they just seem to understand that kids will party and need a safe place, no matter what adults say, so they don't ask a lot of questions. As long as Amanda gets good grades she can do what she wants, and they're pretty open about the cabin when someone needs a place to crash, as long as it's left clean, so I didn't feel like I was being a criminal or anything.

What I was doing didn't seem to involve much real danger. If I got caught, I could always say I was on an adventure to see what it was like being someone else for a few days, and that I planned to write about it. The writing part at least ended up being true, since it's what I'm doing now. Even if I don't get journal page credit for it, I like writing. It helps me think. The game has gone on for more than a few days and now it has become very real.

When I first got here, I made a point of not reading the newspapers or watching TV, so I don't even know the media version of what happened at home. I did write Natalie a note and put it in an addressed envelope with a U.S. stamp and gave it to this friend of Trudy's who came into the restaurant a lot when I first started working there. She went to Hawaii with her son and his family, and I asked her to mail it from there. Everyone at home should know by now I'm not dead, but they'll be looking in the wrong place.

I took some money out of Sterling's savings account with the debit card they gave me, but I don't feel bad about it. I didn't even have to steal the card. They gave it to me on what I thought was my sixteenth birthday. They knew they could trust me not to blow money. I didn't really need anything. They gave me the car and a gas card and an allowance. The debit card was for "just in case," and they knew I would never use it unless there was a real emergency. Sterling has plenty. I used a cash machine at the supermarket near the I-5 on-ramp before I parked the car at the mall, and I cut up the card after I got here so I wouldn't be tempted. Using it again would have led them to me immediately. I didn't take that much and, added to what I had been able to put away, it's been enough. Now I have the job, so I'm not spending much of the money I brought.

It was a real emergency, even though I know they'll never understand. It's like they think that by giving me a comfortable life with nice things, they are taking care of me. But it didn't feel right, and now that I'm away from it, I've come to realize that I can't remember a time when it was right, when I felt close to my mother, and being around Sterling has always felt like ice water. I don't really care what he thinks, but I know Bonnie does. He gives her this life that she wants or needs, and I've been very afraid of disappointing Bonnie. I mean really afraid, like there's some memory I can't pull up from some place I don't want to go again. I'm so afraid, I will do anything to avoid a confrontation, and have lived very carefully by her rules because I believe I know what will happen if I change. But I have already changed. I've been changing for a long time. I have this terror of what she will do when she finally sees it.

I read this book called *The Color of Water*, a true story written by this Black guy whose mom was Jewish. When her family found out she was married to a Black man, they disowned her, with a funeral and everything, like she was dead to them. That's the way Bonnie and Sterling make me feel, like as long as I'm living their way, they'll provide a comfortable life, but if I quit going to church and start getting bad grades, they'll break off any connection altogether. I guess I've decided that they'll be happier believing I'm dead than having to live with the real me walking around as a blemish on their lives. That's what I probably became when Natalie got my note.

I decided to leave the car at the mall in Burlington. It's close to I-5 and I thought it would make them think I went to Seattle or Vancouver. When I first began to have the fantasy, back before I found the bike and it started getting real, I thought I would go to Vancouver. I probably could have driven there in Bonnie's car. Kids go there all the time because the drinking age is nineteen.

Carloads of kids from Western cross over every weekend, and at the border all they want to see is a birth certificate and some picture ID. Having the car would be nice, but it would have made me too visible and easy to find. I needed some time to myself in a new place, the kind of time people get in dry-out clinics or hospitals after they have a breakdown. I haven't come completely unglued yet, though finding the birth certificate made me come close. And now Grant has me hanging out over the edge.

The birth certificate was a total blindside, but one that validated what I was feeling anyway. I wasn't even really snooping, at least not at first. Bonnie has these black pearl earrings that I love. She's really clothes-conscious and spends a lot of money on her looks. It's one of the few ways we've tried to bond. She likes to take me shopping and she has good taste if you want to look like that. She's really girly and because of her, I guess, I have that side, but it's something I learned and it doesn't come from inside me. But that day the earrings were the perfect compliment to what I was wearing and I wanted to find them. She and Sterling had gone to Seattle, so I went into their room and looked in her jewelry box. She does let me wear her stuff, and I had seen her go to that drawer before to add her little touch. Otherwise I wouldn't have snooped.

The earrings weren't in the top tier of the box. It's big and has tiers like for fishing tackle, so I lifted the top layer. Still no black pearls. I started looking for something else that would work and saw the end of this envelope sticking out from underneath the box. I'm not sure what made me do it; just plain curiosity, I guess. I was alone in the house, not in a huge hurry, and I pulled out the envelope. It wasn't sealed, and on it, in Bonnie's handwriting, the words "birth certificate" were written in pencil. Inside, I found this official-looking document that was from Canada and it had my name, Kristen, as the middle name, but a different last name, MacKenzie, which even sounds Canadian. So instead of being

Kristen Adrienne Nichols, I'm suddenly Amy Kristen MacKenzie. It sent chills down my spine, really—like now I know where that saying comes from.

The birth date was different too, like a year-and-a-half before mine, which makes me nineteen now and seems old, like I should already be in college. I don't feel nineteen, and it makes me wonder where that time went. It makes me wonder how Bonnie got the birth certificate she used for me to get my driver's license. Maybe the same way I got the fake license I'm using now.

I was at this party in Bellingham with Natalie and there were some kids from our town there. That's how we knew about it. It was down below the college towards the main part of town and Cellophane Square. Most of the houses in that area are rented by students. I was sitting on this nasty couch that smelled like old beer, and a guy was trying to impress me, hitting on me. He and these other nerd guys were all talking about fake ID. He brought me some pizza and asked me if I wanted a drink from the vodka bottle they were passing around, then showed me this driver's license that had his picture on it.

"Are you really twenty-one?" I asked. He showed me another license that looked identical, but had a birth date that made him nineteen. "What does one of those cost?"

"Depends on who you are and who you know," he said.

So I asked more questions, like could you change the name, and he said you could, but it was harder and would cost more. So I paid him to get me one with the name Amy Kristen MacKenzie on it and the birth date from the Canadian birth certificate. He thought I was crazy for not having it say I was twenty-one, and said I could pass easily if I dressed older. I said I just thought it would be cool to have and I might use it to go clubbing in Canada with my friends, but that I didn't drink that much (true) and thought it was stretching it to say I was that old. So he got me the license and it got me here.

The Canadian Customs guy at the ferry dock in Sidney hardly looked at it. The picture was of the old me and doesn't look much like I look now, so I was relieved, but I think if you look closely enough you could tell it's me. The line was short and everyone else in it was on vacation, so I fit right in with my bike and backpack. I had the birth certificate and license in my hand, ready. He took them from me, but it seemed like he was just doing it because I had them out. He glanced at the birth certificate and said, "Canadian citizen?'

I said, "Yes."

"But you live in the U.S.?"

"My mom's a U. S. citizen."

"Purpose of your visit?"

"To see my dad."

Then he asked me what seemed like memorized questions about what I was bringing, like did I have any weapons or presents for anyone, which I didn't. Then he said, "Have a nice stay," and handed my birth certificate and driver's license back to me and turned his attention to the person in line behind me. He didn't ask about the bike or to look in my pack. I don't know what I expected to happen.

I hadn't slept much in the back seat of Bonnie's car at the mall. I was afraid the security guard would come around and shine his light in the car, but he didn't. I might have slept an hour total, dozing for short periods. It was late when I got done with the change-over at Amanda's cabin and the SKAT bus leaves really early, so I only had a few hours to kill. I knew I had to be at the ferry terminal before 7:30, since the ferry leaves at 7:45.

The big challenge was getting from the mall in Burlington to the ferry dock which is way out by Washington Park, like five miles past Anacortes, and the simplest thing would have been to leave the car at the park or even in Anacortes, but that would have been a giveaway, and I was counting on them not thinking I'm here in Victoria. This whole thing has been pretty surreal. I mean it had way too many parts to it to work, but I didn't worry about it all that much because I hadn't committed any crime or anything, so if I got caught it wasn't going to be the end of the world.

But it did work. Now I wish they would find me so I wouldn't have to make the decision myself to go back.

I was planning to take the bus from Mount Vernon to Anacortes and was riding my bike along Burlington Mall Boulevard towards the new bus terminal in Mount Vernon, trying to get there in time to catch the first bus. It was still dark and there were hardly any cars, and any cop that went by might stop me just to ask what I was doing, riding in the dark, so I had a story ready. The bus driver was my big worry because the busses are nearly empty in the morning, and even though I look way different, I would have to take the bike helmet off and the driver would likely remember me because of having to deal with the bike. It might have created a reason to look for me in Victoria.

It was a complicated plan, and it was totally strange, the way it worked out. I was on the bike near Home Depot, getting close to the Burlington side of the bridge, when this pickup pulls alongside me like I did with Corey that night he took me to his campsite. The passenger window was open, and it was this old guy who lives on Natalie's street.

"Want a ride?"

I could tell he had been drinking, and he didn't seem to recognize me. He's like old enough to be my grandfather. In fact his granddaughters go to my school. One of his front teeth is missing and he would look scary if you'd never seen him before, but he comes to a lot of school sports. Everyone seems to like him, so I didn't panic.

"I'm all right," I said. I wanted him to go away and not attract attention to me.

"A young girl like you shouldn't be on the road by yourself in the dark. There are bad people out here."

"I'm all right," I said. "I do this all the time."

"Put your bike in the back. I'll take you home. You could get hurt."

"I'm not going home. How do I know you won't hurt me?"

"I have granddaughters like you, and I'm no good that way anyway. I mean I couldn't hurt you, but someone else that could might come along here. Let me take you home."

So I stopped, and he stopped the truck and I put the bike in the back and got in.

"Where do you live?"

"I'm not going home. I'm going to work. I work in Anacortes at a hotel, cleaning rooms. My car is broken and I'll lose my job if I don't show up. I was going to take the back roads."

"I'll take you there."

The truck was about the same year as Natalie's aunt's Grenada. The muffler was loud and you could smell the exhaust, but he kept his window open for the air, making it freezing in the cab. He didn't cross the bridge but turned onto the road that goes along the dike behind Home Depot.

"This is the shortest way," he said to reassure me, like he expected me to be afraid of being off the main road with him. He got on Highway 20 before the Shell, scaring me with the way he let the truck wander in and out of the lane. I was sure we would be stopped, but we weren't. In Anacortes, he pulled off the highway onto the road that runs toward the marina through the industrial park.

"Where do you want me to let you off?"

"By the Safeway," I said. "Since you gave me a ride, I'm early and have time to get something to eat."

"Young girls shouldn't be out alone like this. You tell your father he should give you a ride."

"He would if he could," I said. "You're a nice man. Thank you."

I don't think he recognized me, and the rest was easy. It was daylight by then and the road out to the ferry is straight with only a few hills. The shoulder has a bike lane or sidewalk most of the way and the traffic wasn't heavy yet. Since the ferries go through the San Juans, stopping at the big islands where bicycling is popular, a person on a bicycle heading toward the dock is a common enough sight and doesn't attract attention. I got there with plenty of time to spare and even sat in the warmth of the waiting room until it was time to board, too tired to think much about anything. I didn't see anyone I knew, but I didn't really care. I was just putting one foot in front of the other to see how far I could get.

I had been on those ferries several times before with the school. We play soccer with both Friday Harbor and Orcas. Waiting for the ferry seemed normal and I bought the same onion bagel with cream cheese I always buy. Only this time I had coffee too, with cream in it.

It was about 7:00 when I got there, so I didn't have to wait long. It's funny how sometimes you make decisions that end up being important just because someone assumes she knows what you will do. I rode up to the ticket booth on the bike and the woman inside assumed I was taking it, so she charged me for it and I paid even though the bike seemed like a complication, extra baggage that I hadn't thought of as anything but a way to get to the ferry dock. I knew I could get a bus from Sidney to Victoria, but wasn't sure they would let me bring the bike and didn't know if I wanted to ride it that far or what the roads would be like.

The trip through the islands is beautiful. It was the weekend. There were sailboats and seagulls and sun, and that wonderful smell of saltwater that makes it feel like summer, so I just went with it. I followed the other walk-on passengers up the steel gangplank and through Customs and found myself pushing a bicycle in Sidney, British Columbia, less than three hours from home, but in a different country, a different world. In my pack I had a few changes of clothes. I had money in my pocket and I looked like someone I hardly recognized in the mirror.

Without the bike, I wouldn't have met Grant.

Corey

Okay, so I've been in here way too long now. The novelty has clearly worn off. It has sucked from the moment the sheriff's car showed up by the sewer treatment plant the morning after she disappeared, but time went by faster in the beginning. Even if it was in a very bad way, I was treated like a kind of celebrity and got a lot of attention. Most of the time they were pretty polite, but not always. Sometimes they were downright mean, and lied to trick me into confessing. Considering what they think I've done, it's understandable, and I've thought about confessing. Just like suicide, confessing a lie is a real option, but I haven't done either yet.

They haven't formally charged me. The public defender lawyer they've assigned me says it may happen soon. If it doesn't, they'll have to let me out. They don't know what to charge me with. They haven't found Kristen's body, so all they really know is that she's gone. The evidence they have against me is all circumstantial. They found her socks with some blood on them and her hair on a fleece at the river campsite, so they know she was there at some time, but that doesn't prove I raped her or killed her, even if they believe I did. My fingerprints and a lot of other people's were in her car, but I don't have the money that was taken from the cash machine by someone using her stepdad's debit card.

Mainly, they think I'm scum and they can connect me to her and they need someone to blame to make their world feel safe again. I don't have a good alibi, and I was seen walking alone on the road between the highway and town when she was supposed to be headed home.

Because it's the truth, my story doesn't change, but they keep trying. And even though they do break the monotony of being here, I dread the sessions where they quiz me over and over to try to make me crack. They're so sure I did it. That's the hardest part. Everyone believes it. I bet even Smith believes it. How could he help it? I know Harold believes it. And my mom probably wishes it wasn't true, but feels like it's one more way her life has gone bad and blames my dad and his drinking. They've both been here to see me, my mom and dad, separately. For both visits they let us be in a room together, but with a guard just outside the door. There's a camera mounted from the ceiling, but at least we didn't have to talk on a phone through glass.

When my dad came it was in the morning, so he was still relatively sober, but I could smell alcohol over his Altoid breath. I know from staying at his house that he starts the day with a snort. He drinks vodka because he doesn't think anybody can smell it, and when either my sister or I am around, he keeps it in a cupboard in the kitchen. When he wakes up, he goes straight to it. He manages a daily routine and still has a job. He sells roofing at a wholesale warehouse and they keep him around, even though he drinks on the sly there too, because he knows a lot about roofing. He used to own a bigger company than the one he works at now, back when he and my mom were still married.

When he came, we made small talk and he asked if they were treating me all right. He's pretty nonjudgmental, like he didn't make me feel worse, the way my mom does, by dumping the grief and embarrassment being related to me causes him on top of the load of problems I already have. But his life is such a mess that his attempts at support don't mean much. He talked about my older sister who he said was doing okay, but I'm sure would be doing better without a big murder scandal involving her brother. I hardly listen to what he says anymore because he's never been much help, so I just look at his eyes. They're always sad, and I wonder what happened in his life that made him quit trying. I wonder a lot whether trying is worth much.

His visit was pretty painless. At least it wasn't excruciating like when my mom came. She just looked at me and burst out crying. Like I needed that on top of what I'm already facing. She's done it before, a lot. I make her cry. My sister makes her cry. My dad makes her cry. So it wasn't a surprise, but it was different this time. It was like the grand finale, the overload, the you've-caused-me-more-grief-than-I-could-ever-bear-or-even-imagine-bearing cry.

There wasn't anything to say, but she felt obligated to stay around for a while. It had the effect of making me feel even worse. We sat across the table from each other. I couldn't do much but look at my hands lying on the tabletop. I didn't know where else to put them. Even though I wanted to scream that I didn't do it, I didn't say anything, but waited to see what she would say. But she just looked at me until a wave of tears and sobs overtook her. I'm sure my hands on the table didn't help. They probably looked like weapons, considering what she thinks I did. I must seem like a monster to her, one that came from her body like in a bad science fiction movie, and it's just all too much to handle.

She never did manage to say anything, nor did she touch me, not even a pat on the shoulder. Not that I expected it or, at the time, thought I wanted it. But later, after she left, I figured out that I really did want it, did want her to say something nice, like she believed in me, or touch me. If she had so much as patted my hand or shoulder, I would have lost it and cried too. But as it turned out, the image of me as a monster stayed, and her visit was a bad experience for both of us.

They're holding me here on technical stuff now that has nothing to do with Kristen. Drug charges, actually. The lawyer lady says they can't keep me here forever without filing formal charges about Kristen, so they may have to let me out, at least for a while, which should make me happy, but instead it scares me.

After they picked me up that morning, they searched my room and found my stash. I really don't smoke that much, or at least I didn't before all this, but a lot of kids at school do. I don't have a regular job because I can't drive but, like everyone, I need money. Anyway, this business opportunity presented itself. I've had jobs before. I'm not lazy, and sometimes I do yard work that I get by answering ads that are posted on a board outside the attendance office at school, or there are some guys who graduated a few years ago who have a business doing yard work, and when they get too much work, they call me.

So I had some money saved. A few hundred dollars. I was thinking about a car, like maybe my dad would let me put it on his insurance or something, since working with Harold and my mom on that project is out of the question. Anyway, my dad got another DUI and now he has to prove he's sober by blowing into this breathalyzer tube that has been installed in his car. He's always having the kid next door or one of the kids who loads trucks at his job blow in the tube so he can start the car. He drinks and drives anyway, and I figure it would take a million bucks to get his insurance company to add his kid who has already had an MIP. So I gave up on the car idea and when I got an opportunity to buy some weed, well. . . I'm pretty disciplined about stuff like that and also pretty discreet. I figured I could triple my money over time by selling a few joints here and there, like when I needed money for a movie or beer, and it was working pretty well until this happened.

So they're holding me on a drug charge which wouldn't keep me here overnight if anyone wanted me out, but no one does. And maybe that's the truly sobering and sad part of all this. I mean I want out. I didn't hurt Kristen. I miss her and I hate it here. I'm in a cage. The food is crappy. The days are boring.

Having cancer would be easier. I want out of here so bad I get lightheaded thinking about it, but I've got no place to go.

I read a lot in here, and have actually been doing some schoolwork. They have this school counselor who is maybe the only kind person here. She checked my school records. My school has one of the highest graduation requirements around, but she figured out that even though there's no chance I can graduate from my school with my class, if I work at it, I could meet the minimum requirements for a diploma from the state, which are lower, and actually graduate at the same time my class does. Even though I don't feel much hope about next year or next week or, especially, graduation, I don't want to hurt her feelings, so I do some schoolwork. It passes the time. Although I'm good at fantasizing and can lose myself in my imagination, you can't do it all day and night without weed or something to help, so I guess I'm using schoolwork like weed, as an escape. What a weird thought.

A person has to be realistic, and even with my good imagination, I know the difference between pretending and reality. The truth is that my future is at least as messed up as my present. When the lawyer first said something about them letting me out, I got excited. All I could think about was being away from here. I thought about the campsite by the river, about walking in the night, about getting stoned, hanging at the beach, walking in the woods, sunlight.

Then I really thought about it. No one wants me out. No one would trust me. There's no way in hell I could stay with my mom and Harold. So that leaves my dad. I could stay there; ironically, now they would let me. If I could go back in time to before Kristen disappeared, but keep what I've learned from being stuck in here, maybe I could make it work, but not now. I'm a friggin outcast. I know myself well enough to know that it won't take me long to blow and do something that will put me back in here. And I could easily hurt someone.

So I'm just waiting for them to figure out that I'm telling the truth, and maybe the best place to wait is here. Sometimes I daydream about Kristen, have conversations with her. I imagine that she's safe somewhere, free. I imagine myself camping with her on a beach in Mexico. There was a feeling about her, like she understood isolation, and she's the only person I know who I think would get it, my situation, the aloneness of it, I mean. She would understand.

I also think a lot about getting stoned, which is probably more realistic than the chance of Kristen being alive or me being cleared. I know it's a cop-out. My dad is my dad. I have a cop-out for a role model. But I crave, and crave is the right word, that comfortable, numb feeling, even if it is fake and comes from chemicals. I just want freedom, freedom from knowing that my life has spun out of control and may be unfixable and that I'm responsible for some of it. I know I've done my share of fucking up, but I didn't hurt her. I didn't kill her. I might even be in love with her. And I don't think I want to die yet, but I go back and forth with it. Right now, I just want to escape from the way it feels to be me, and if I had the right drugs... Like the song says, "All the money in the world's spent on feeling good."

Kristen

Before Grant got scary, I liked it here. Even with the messiness, it feels so much more real than life with Bonnie and Sterling. In a way, this house is a lot like Natalie's, kind of ghetto, but I don't expect anything from it except a dry place to sleep, and no one is pretending it's anything else. The house is a dump and Sterling would call my roommates losers, but they don't steal my stuff or scare me, and we're becoming friends. I met them in a pub downtown a couple of blocks back from the harbor my first night. We kept bumping into each other around town after that, and now I live with them.

If I miss anything, it's talking to Natalie. She thought my life was pretty good. I think her life feels pretty bad too and our being friends allowed her to share the things I had which gave her a kind of hope, so I didn't talk to her about my escape fantasy. I had things she wants but can't get right now, like a car and a nice house. American dream kind of stuff that I've always had, but have abandoned now because when you do have it and all the valves are shut, it still feels like a drippy cement box. I envy her, which is ironic. She can talk to her Aunt Trish and you can feel actual warmth in their house, even though it's on the rez.

Today is one of those dark, wet spring days, and the raindrop splattering is jiggling the leaves on the few mangy shrubs in the yard. Sitting here is depressing anyway, but if I could push Grant out of my mind, it would be okay. The kitchen stinks of stale beer, no one has dumped the garbage, and the ashtrays are full. The house is just plain grimy. Sometimes I clean it, but I don't feel like it today. Maybe it's the rain. Outside, water's dripping from the gutters that must have been plugged up all winter, because the trees have only recently leafed out again. I've been here a couple of months, and even though the kitchen is a mess, at least I'm comfortable with my roommates.

One of the good things here is the park, which isn't that far away and goes on forever. It's called Dallas Road. It's on the Strait of Juan de Fuca, which is not as wide as the English Channel, but is a serious gulf that separates me from that other life. I'm in a different country, yet on a clear day, I can see across to the Olympic Mountains. The park follows the water for miles and it's quite beautiful, with duck ponds, lawns, rhododendrons, madrona trees and a walkway on a high bluff with a great view. There are places where you can get to the beach, and sometimes I just sit for hours and watch the waves break, even when it's cold.

But the park is where I met Grant, so I don't go there anymore.

The other good thing is Trudy. She's this woman where I work. It's a crappy job, at least as bad as Natalie's toilet cleaning at the Cormorant. Trudy helped me get hired when, right after I got here, I was eating there a lot because the food is cheap and not that bad. Trudy reminds me a little of Natalie's Aunt Trish. Not that they look alike, but she has this warmth about her that makes me look forward to the times when we work together.

After I met Trudy and got the job and found this place to stay, I felt this huge easing of pressure. I could finally sleep at night. Now I lie awake. When a car goes by or parks on our street, I'm sure it's the white Escalade. When I don't hear anything, it's worse; I'm sure he's lurking outside my window.

It was the poetry, Emily Dickinson and Walt Whitman, that gave me the push. You may be thinking that there's something bad about poetry that could make someone who'd been doing all the right things flip out and disappear. But I don't see anything bad about it at all. It was such a surprise to find it right there in

a school textbook where you wouldn't expect anything but more
noise to help you pass the state test or get a good-paying job, even
if the job's pointless.

As if money is all there is to life! It was such a relief to learn
I'm not the only one who has ever had those kinds of thoughts.
And it wasn't just some other crazy kid, but these famous old
poets whose poems ended up in a book that kids everywhere
have to read. Besides, it wasn't only the poems.

Leaving wasn't a choice.

Even after all those years living in that house, talking with
Bonnie and Sterling every day, I never could connect with them.
I tried, but they didn't touch me, not the part of me that counts.
All the water that came through their faucets was freezing.
Remember the valve image I described? I picture myself alone in
this cement box, like a big bathtub or a tomb, all cold, damp and
drippy with a bunch of faucets sticking through the cement, and
if you open Bonnie's or Sterling's faucet, the water that comes
out is so cold that you can hardly stand it. I couldn't go on giving
them my words and my life. I gave it my best shot for as long as I
could. I really did want to die. The poems may be what saved me.

But there were also a few other things.

I was watching the news on TV with some of the other ASB
kids at Leslie's house. We had been planning the Martin Luther
King Day assembly for school. Anyway, there was this news
story about one of the coaches of an NBA team whose eighteen-
year-old son had committed suicide. The story didn't deal at all
with the kid, just the famous dad and how everyone felt bad for
him and was praying for him. Then Leslie said something and it
stuck. She's not the deepest person, so I don't expect things she
says to stick, let alone influence major choices, but this one did.
She said she couldn't imagine wanting to kill yourself, which I
can believe, but then she said,

"Why didn't he just leave? I mean why would you kill

yourself? That's so final. The guy was eighteen. He could just leave if he wanted to. No one could stop him."

She was right. It is so final.

So between Leslie and Whitman and Emily, I had a lot to think about. Then I found myself hearing things from other unlikely sources, like Corey. I'll talk more about him later, but for now I'll just say it was building up inside. I was living all the motions of that life, but underneath, I had this fantasy going, like when you're a kid playing with dolls or stuffed animals. I've seen boys do it too, with action figures. You imagine this whole alternate world with its own story playing out. I imagined just leaving. And I started to do things, set up props, like I did with my stuffed animals when I was little. The bike was the first prop.

It's how I met Grant.

It's an older road bike, silver with skinny tires and a French name, Peugeot, like the car, and nothing on it was broken or missing. I could have ridden it away. I was driving to Anacortes alone from Natalie's, on the back road along the beach where there are a lot of expensive houses. Leaning against a gatepost at the end of a driveway there was this bike with a sign on it that said, "Free." The decision was spur-of-the-moment, not really a commitment, though it ended up being a turning point because it was the first real thing I did and it made it easier to keep fantasizing about the plan.

I hid the bike in this old shed behind Amanda's family beach house. There's a road along the beach that runs out to a point called "Pull and Be Damned" because back in the day, some guy had to row a boat around it to get to town and the tidal current made the rowing hard. Anyway, the property out there belongs to the tribe and is leased to white people for beach houses. Since the land is leased, people don't like to build expensive houses, so there are mostly summer homes and some of the kids at school have cabins there. Amanda is also in the ASB crowd and sometimes has parties at the cabin when the adults are gone. There's this old, fallen-down shed in the woods between the cabin and the road, and I put the bike in the shed, thinking because it was free, it wouldn't matter if it was found, but it might come in handy in my plan.

That was when I was starting to get to know Corey. Natalie hates him because of this video camera incident. She and I have never talked about it, but I've heard about it in great detail from other people. He taped her from a closet at a party while she was having sex with this jerk. Then she smashed the tape. I know it makes him sound creepy, but I don't get creepiness from him and I think they were both being stupid in different ways, and if she could learn from it, so could he. Anyway, he has this real alone side, like Emily Dickinson. He even has this cool campsite out on the river with a tent and stuff hidden where he can go to escape his stepdad. He took me there and told me a story about his uncle. I think hearing the story was the tipping point.

His uncle had a rebellious stage when he was young, like Corey. His parents were pretty strict and made him work for the family construction business whenever he wasn't doing a sport after school, and on Saturdays and all summer. They paid him but wouldn't let him spend the money. He wanted to buy a nice car and could afford it, but had to put nearly all the money he made in the bank to save for college or to buy a house or something. He got this small allowance for movies, burgers and clothes, but he had to beg to use the family car, which was this old-lady, four-door Buick.

So one day he was at the bank depositing his paycheck like he was supposed to, and the teller, who was a girl not much older than him, made a comment about how much money he had saved and how cool she thought it was. He said he'd buy a car if he could, but he couldn't take any of it out. She said she'd go to Hawaii if she had that much money, but it was probably good that he was saving it.

He kept the bankbook in the same kitchen drawer at home where it had been kept since he started working when he was ten or so and old enough to do clean-up around a building site. His parents could look at it whenever they wanted, and kept track of how much he had. Up until that moment he was talking with the teller, he had thought it was impossible to get the money out of the account without his dad's signature, but now it occurred to him that he didn't know that for sure, so he asked. She told him it was a joint account and that either he or his dad could withdraw from it, but it only took one signature.

Back then you could do a lot of things you can't do now, like buy a car without your parent's signature, and he was able to divert enough money from his pay to buy an old Chevy for a hundred and fifty bucks from a kid at school. He parked the car at a supermarket parking lot half a mile from his house. He would leave home in the morning, saying he was going to catch a ride with a friend up the street, then walk to his car and drive to school. His school was huge, not like ours where everyone would notice and it would get back to your parents the first day. Eventually he got caught and of course there was a huge fight, and he was grounded forever, but it didn't stop him. He had learned a lot about what you can do over the telephone from watching his parents run their business. From TV he knew enough to make the key calls from the pay phone at the supermarket.

He was really pissed and he had all that money in the bank and he knew he could get it just by going in there and signing for it. He also knew it wouldn't take long for his parents to find out after he got the money, so he needed a plan. His family had been to Hawaii, which was a big deal back then; the construction company did pretty well sometimes and when it did, they celebrated with a vacation. So he knew how to buy plane tickets.

While he was on restriction, he had time to scheme and work

out the details of the plan. He didn't tell anyone, not even his closest friends, because he knew that as soon as he disappeared, they'd be questioned. The amount of planning he did was amazing. He got his money out by making a big show at the bank, saying his parents had finally agreed to let him buy a car. He even described it. It actually existed on a lot nearby where he'd talked to a salesman about it.

So he ran away to Hawaii and lived on the beach and bummed around for three or four weeks before he got caught. He might not have gotten caught if he hadn't sent a post card to one of his friends. Either the parents of the kid he sent it to intercepted it, or the kid talked. Corey's uncle's parents were worried the way you'd expect them to be, and they made a big fuss about how he might be dead or kidnapped, but they knew he was pissed and that he took the money, so they and the cops strongly suspected that he had run away.

While Corey was telling the story all I could think about was how I had been doing all this secret escape planning myself, like a fantasy game in my head. Hearing about someone who had actually made it happen allowed me to take a pretty significant step forward.

That, and finding the birth certificate.

The birth certificate was huge. I mean it was bad enough, feeling disconnected from my mom and her life with Sterling, but finding out that I have a completely different last name that nobody had ever mentioned, and that I'm not even an American citizen, and that I'm a year and a half older than I thought I was, about blew me away. I felt like downing a bottle of Sterling's scotch, flooring the Taurus on Reservation Road and letting the steering wheel go, but I didn't.

Instead, I took Leslie's advice, played out my fantasy like Corey's uncle did and put the birth certificate to use. I haven't cut myself once since I left, and I don't have to fight off the urge to let the car veer into a tree or power pole or off a cliff, because I don't have a car. Maybe this isn't better, but it feels real and it's not final.

Not yet, anyway.

Natalie

It's strange how losing someone can make you feel. The significant people I've lost in my life are my dad (he died last year), Kristen (you know her story), and also my mom. My mom is alive, but she's pretty much missing from my life. She still calls once in a while. Last time it was from Florida, the day after Christmas. She was drunk and full of excuses for not sending a present, and promises that she would never make good on. My dad was never around, but I used to fantasize about him coming to fix my life. It was pretty much a pipe dream. He was a loser too. When I heard my dad died—he was murdered—I didn't feel much. Maybe I'm holding it inside and am screwed up in my subconscious, but when someone was never present, it's hard to muster much real emotion when you learn his absence is permanent. I think I gave up on the dream version of my dad long before he died. But that's all he ever was to me anyway—a dream.

My mom has been harder to let go of because I lived with her when I was young and you make those attachments, you bond, but I've been with Aunt Trish for so long now, and she's the person who has been there for me when I needed someone, that I don't miss my mom anymore. If she disappeared entirely, I would feel bad for a while, but I wouldn't feel her as an actual absence from my life. I wouldn't be reminded of her every day when I was just doing normal stuff. There wouldn't be this big hole in my life, the way there is now, with Kristen missing from it. The worst part is not knowing what happened. I really miss her.

I trust instincts, gut feelings. I can't pin down a feeling about

Kristen. Sometimes I get the big sadness, grief, about her, and I just feel stuck, like nothing matters anymore. I used to tell her nearly everything. The few things I held back weren't because I thought she wouldn't understand, but because I just didn't want to go there. Like I never told her the blow-by-blow about Corey and the camera, and now I think I should have. It might have saved her. Sometimes I get this light, good feeling about her, like she's out there somewhere doing fine and I don't need to be sad. I've heard about people having dreams after someone they're close to dies. The person comes and talks to them in a dream and says or does something that allows them to let go. Kristen hasn't come to me yet, and I haven't let go.

I keep wanting to call her up so we can talk, because that's what I always did when something important happened. I want to tell her about Brad. It's killing me that this new and crazy thing is happening to me and there's no one to tell. They're probably going to let Corey out of jail in a week or so. It's not really jail, even though he deserves the worst; it's Juvie. He can rape and kill my best friend, but because he's only seventeen, they have to protect him from getting hurt in jail. What a bunch of bull. Now they have to let him out because they haven't found her body, and they can't prove that she's dead or that the weasel bastard did anything, even though we all know he did it. He's been in there for almost two months, and even though they found a lot of pot in his room, that isn't enough to keep him locked up any longer.

They haven't found any new clues and he sticks by his story. They even looked for her body in the drainage ditch next to where Brad and I parked that night. There's all this talk on the news about prisoners' rights in the Iraq war and about whether the government has the right to torture people to get them to talk. I would have said no before all this happened, but if torturing Corey would get him to tell us the truth about what he did to her, they should do it.

Brad came and got me yesterday morning. He was here by ten. We got off I-5 north of Seattle because he said there would be less traffic if we went the back way and avoided the city. I was surprised by how, once we got off the freeway and onto the residential streets on Mercer Island, the neighborhoods were so quiet, like people might have gardens and grow organic vegetables. The road near Brad's house is wooded on both sides, and the houses are spread out. They aren't all mansions or anything, but you can tell people have money.

Brad's family has a ski boat and we spent a great day on the lake. He pulled me around on an inner tube for a while, but I couldn't drive the boat, so he didn't get a turn. Mostly, we just drifted around, talking, and jumped in when we got too hot. We cruised along the shoreline, looking at people's houses and yards for some of the time. There are a lot of rich people on Mercer Island. I have to admit I felt more than a little out of place, and it started to depress me, so I got quiet, which made Brad ask what was wrong. The cool part was I felt that I was able to just come right out and say it. I mean he feels like my friend, and I haven't let myself get any big expectations yet, so I don't have anything to lose. I know he's way out of my league. We live in different worlds. But we have fun together and I feel comfortable with him in a way I've never felt with a guy before, so I just keep saying what I feel. We're having this kind of cross-cultural experiment and it still feels good, even after what happened before he brought me home.

Kristen

Though I didn't expect to have a bike here, I've used it a lot. The part of this city I move around in most is made for a bike. It's pretty flat between the house and the park, and between the house and work only the last few blocks are uphill. Some streets are really congested and riding can be a little dangerous, but it's a pretty good way to get around and a lot of people ride, so I don't feel out of place.

There are always better bikes nearby when I have to leave mine parked in a rack downtown or at the park, so if someone is looking to steal one, he wouldn't choose mine, but I bought a good lock anyway. The bike has special significance, like my Garfield doll when I was a kid. It has brought me luck, both kinds. It's worked both as transportation and as a prop for the role I'm playing, the character I've had to become.

I've definitely changed. I think about going back, and sometimes I imagine the end-of-year stress and excitement at school, and the Valley, and driving around in Bonnie's Taurus. My old life seems like another dimension, not very real and a million light years away, the way Corey described his sense of going to college. Here, I go to work at the restaurant and the rest of my time is my own to manage for better or worse.

I'm sort of pretending my life is a play. The part I had in the play at school last year was only a few lines, but while we were rehearsing, I listened to Mrs. Packard talking to some of the other actors about how you get into character. It all ties in with this being like one of those kid fantasies that has become real. I've gotten used to this role I'm living, and it's gotten easier to stay in character.

At the restaurant, I have different hours each week and I don't always work the same shift as Trudy, but I see her often enough and she helps me feel like I'm part of a team. The work gets hectic during rush times and I'm glad when the shift is over. It isn't something I imagine myself doing for very long, but I don't hate it. The customers seem to like me and the tips aren't bad. All in all, it's not that hard. I get to feel like I belong when I'm at the restaurant, and knowing in the back of my head that it's temporary may be what has helped me to keep from feeling that I'm trapped in a crappy job, the way I would if I was Trudy's age.

At first, when I wasn't at work, I would hang out with my roommates, Ian and Char. I liked going to bars with them. It was like a party scene, only in a bar instead of at someone's house. It could be pretty expensive even at the cheap places we went, but I don't drink much, and because I'm a girl sometimes guys would buy for me. I started to get to know a few people, not like I was making real friends, but there were faces I'd recognize, people I'd say hi to. Even so, I still spent a lot of time alone.

I went to the history museum. There's so much there you can't take it all in without going back, but it is too expensive, so I just went once. By the entrance to the harbor where the park ends, there's this giant cement breakwater that protects the ships and barges that come to be loaded or unloaded at the big warehouse on the dock. You can walk out to the end of the breakwater, and on the ocean side, the open water changes moods with the weather. On the sheltered side, over at the dock, there's usually a lot of noise and activity, with forklifts racing around and men shouting. I love walking out to the end of the breakwater. When it's not windy, I see a lot of mothers and grandmothers pushing baby carriages. Being next to the ocean gives you this sense of being lonely and sort of melancholy, only happy, and it feels safe.

The park runs along the water for miles and most of the time feels like a family place. When the weather's good, people jog, walk their dogs, ride their bikes. Families go for walks in the evening. I've spent a lot of time there. Most of the park is on a bluff above the beach, but there are some stretches of beach with stairs going down to it. At high tide there isn't much exposed, but at low tide you can have a nice walk between two of the stairways. I sit on a log or on the gravel with my back against a log and look at the water. It calms me. But I'm obviously not the only one who gets something good from it.

I wasn't a dedicated jogger back in the Valley, but before Grant, I went jogging a lot here. I even bought some running shoes with tip money. They were on sale and aren't anything I would wear in the Valley, but they suit the new me just fine. I would ride the bike to the park and lock it into one of the racks, then go for a run. Sometimes I sat on the beach first, before I got sweaty. The day my bike broke, I had done that. It was a grey day, kind of misty, and you couldn't see across the Strait. There was a little breeze but no rain yet, and I got cold just sitting so I didn't stay long. I like moody, dark days almost as much as bright, sunny ones, but I don't like being cold, so I climbed back up the stairs and jogged the mile or so to the lighthouse at the east end of the park. There's a hill to climb coming back, so I was pretty tired when I got on the bike.

When I was sitting on the beach I was wearing a dark blue anorak. I'm pretty conscientious and don't leave things lying around or lose things very often, but I must have been distracted. By the time I got to the lighthouse I'd worked up a sweat, so I took the windbreaker off and sat down at one of the picnic tables to catch my breath. Then I left without it. I wore it a lot and didn't want to spend another thirty dollars for a new one, so I went back on the bike. Luckily, it was still there.

I had to pump hard to get the bike back up the hill and needed to shift to a lower gear or get off and walk. The bike is the old kind of ten-speed that doesn't click to let you know when the chain is lined up to shift, and I'm not very good at judging since I wasn't a bike rider before. There were people around and I didn't want to embarrass myself by having to get off and push, so I tried to shift while I was pedaling hard. Well, the chain jumped off the front sprocket. This would have been bad enough, but then it got caught between the pedal crank and the frame as I was pushing down with all my weight.

It broke. I mean it really broke; instead of it being a loop that I could try to put back on, it was one long piece with loose ends. I came down pretty hard. Luckily it's a girl's bike with no bar to hit, but my foot slipped off the pedal, and I rolled my ankle trying to keep from falling. I stayed up, but it hurt. It turned out I had an audience.

I pushed the bike off the road onto the strip of lawn between the curb and the jogging path. My foot was really sore when I put weight on it. The chain fell off and I picked it up and wrapped it around the frame under the seat. I was wiping my hands on the grass to get the grease off them when he said,

"Are you hurt?"

I was pretty preoccupied, so I didn't focus on him right away.

"I'm all right," I said. "The bike's not, but it can probably be fixed."

"How's your ankle? You came down hard. You're limping."

That's when I actually looked at him. He was clearly an adult, probably in his mid to late thirties, and was dressed for jogging, the way you'd expect someone with money to go jogging. He had on nice warm-ups and his running shoes were expensive. I've learned to recognize expensive clothes from shopping with Bonnie. He was good-looking in an old guy, James Bond sort of way.

"Can I give you a lift?" he asked.

"I'll be okay," I said, and I thought I would be, so I raised the kickstand and started pushing the bike up the hill. It was maybe a mile and a half to the house. I didn't look back and didn't think much about him until about ten minutes later when my ankle started to hurt worse. It needed ice, I needed to not be walking on it, and I still had a mile and a quarter to go. So when his white Cadillac SUV pulled up next to me with the window down and he said, "Are you sure I can't take you home?" I said okay.

He had to take the front wheel off the bike to get it in the back, but it came off easily. The car was spotless and the bike wasn't, but he had some clothes from the cleaners hanging behind the driver's seat and he took a couple of the plastic slip covers off and put them under the bike to protect the car from the grease. Aside from his clothes, there were a dress and a woman's blouse on the hangers, so I assumed he was married.

While we were driving, he asked me if I was going to school. I told him I'd graduated and was working at a restaurant for now, but planned to go to university next year. I'd picked that up, the way they say university here instead of college. I ended up saying the name of the restaurant too, which I thought was harmless because it's a public place and not like some big secret or anything. It just seemed part of the conversation. He seemed like this family guy, like he probably had a daughter at home and helping me would somehow make the world safer for her too.

He dropped me off in front of the house. I thanked him and he drove off. I didn't expect to ever see him again.

Corey

They asked me if I wanted to see Smith. They took me to the office of the guy who runs this place, and he said Smith requested it. Since Smith isn't my parent, it wasn't a normal situation, but because he was my teacher, if I wanted him to come, they could let him. I said yes because my first thought was that he was always a fair guy, but after I got back to my room, I was lying on the bunk, staring at the mortar lines between the painted cement blocks that the walls are made of, and I started thinking, and I got kind of paranoid. I started thinking that the cops are probably using him to try to get me to confess. They've tried everything else. They all believe I killed her. It would be easier to confess than to keep telling the truth. Since I don't know what happened and didn't have anything to do with it, I would have to make up a good story. I would have to say I dumped the body out in the bay somewhere, like off the Deception Pass bridge where the water is deep, and it could have drifted out into the Straits where it disappeared. People have jumped from there and have never been seen again.

In a way, it would be easier to confess to Smith than to the cops because it wouldn't feel so much like giving in, like being beaten, like at the end of The Crucible, a play we read in his class. When this guy, John Proctor, confesses to being a witch because that's what people want to hear, and by confessing he gets to live, he tells his wife that it's hard to give a lie to dogs. His honesty matters a lot to him and he's trying to find a way to do right in a really bad situation. Proctor screwed up in a big way, but he wasn't a witch like the judges said, so I'm kind of like him in that way.

But it would be hard to lie to Smith. The cops have lied to me, so lying to them would have a kind of fairness to it. I mean it would be ironic that their feeling of justice and the relief they would get from thinking they had their bad guy and the world was safe again would be based on a lie. He's coming today, Smith, and I'm nervous. My heart is beating too fast, which makes my mouth dry, and my voice will crack if I try to talk, which makes me look guilty as hell. I don't know why I'm getting this way. I mean he's just a teacher and can't really do anything more to me than they've already done.   *

By the way, Proctor tore up his confession and was hung. I don't know if I have that much integrity, and I'm really not very brave, but I'm also not sure what I'm more afraid of, being sent to prison and having my butt reamed every day by some animal or getting out of here and having to live in a world that believes I'm a psycho killer. I think Smith would probably like it that I remembered all the stuff from the play.

Kristen

Thinking about going back makes me think about trying to be Kristin again. It really is just a phone call away, but it seems like a million light years.

From being here, I've learned that if you don't know what to expect, and you don't build up some idea ahead of time about how you want life to be, and just roll with what happens by deciding whether you have any reason to be miserable right now, like are you cold or hungry, or too tired or in pain, most of the time you're either all right or could fix it pretty easily if you want to. Kristen's life felt more like a tangled web of lies than this life does.

I know I don't want Bonnie and Sterling's life. Sterling makes lots of money, but I don't think he's happy, at least not in the way I see happiness or want it for myself. Even though he tries to be nice to me, I don't like him. I don't respect him. It's like his god is money. He and his partners bought up the part of town where there used to be canneries and warehouses. Our town is really small, so the deal isn't as big as this description might make it sound. The part they bought has quite a lot of waterfront but it's zoned wrong for what they want to do, which is build condos and put in more shops, like at Whistler. If they get their way, it will change the town completely. He says it will make it better. A lot of the people who live there like the town the way it is, but since they didn't have the money to buy the property, he says they don't have the right to complain. The hitch is that the project can't be built unless the zoning is changed, and he expects the town to change the zoning for his project. But you can use his logic against him. He knew what he was buying and if he didn't want property that's zoned the way it is, he shouldn't have bought it. Why should they change it?

He probably really believes that the town will be a better place with all the new buildings and businesses and all the new people they will bring, but a lot of people disagree, and Sterling wants to shove his plan down their throats so he can make more money. I've heard him on the phone with his partners and people he thinks are insiders. They're pretty arrogant and sometimes downright nasty. He's completely different with the newspaper and with people who might disagree with him. He can really turn on the charm. He expects Bonnie and me to agree with him because it's his money that pays for the way we live. Bonnie goes along with it, but it's hard for me to tell what she really thinks. Even though I've never said it aloud, I don't buy any of it. I think Sterling is a greedy hypocrite, but he takes care of Bonnie, so I've kept my opinions to myself.

My problem with Bonnie is that it doesn't ever feel like you can touch her, like you're connecting to the soul part of her. I fantasize about someday, maybe after college when I'm on my own, being able to go out to lunch with her, just her, no Sterling, and drink a little wine with her so she'll loosen up. I want her to tell me stories about when she was growing up, about meeting my real dad, and whether she felt all the uncertainty I feel about life. She's my mom, but she's like this big mystery, and instead of helping me figure out how to live, she makes everything more confusing.

We don't fight much. Sometimes I wish we did. Natalie and Trish fight, but it's like they're sisters. They know each other really well and they get over it quickly. I don't feel like I know Bonnie at all. She has never talked about my real dad or about my other stepdad, the one I had when I was little. I must have asked at some time, but I don't remember it. She's an artist at dodging. Before you know what's happening, she's anticipating the question and redirecting the conversation, so there's no good way to ask it. Now I know better than to ask. It's like one of those dog fences that you can't see. I've just learned not to go there. As you can imagine, finding the birth certificate was quite a shock. My real dad might live here in Victoria, or in Vancouver, or he might be dead. It would be nice to know.

Bonnie keeps herself in good shape. She looks great for someone who's nearly forty. She works out at the fitness center at least three times a week and spends a lot on clothes and make-up. Her taste tends to be pretty upscale city and, to me, she often seems overdressed for where we live. But I've learned a lot about clothes from watching her. She runs Sterling's office and seems pretty well educated, meaning her grammar and vocabulary are good and she's good at math, but she lets her religion do all her abstract thinking. (I got that from Smith. He's always talking about the difference between abstract and concrete reality and how the abstractions like love, greed, fear, envy, and things like that drive our lives as much as concrete things like food and shelter.) Bonnie doesn't read writers like Emily Dickinson or Emerson or Thoreau, or even current books like the ones Oprah talks about on her show. I don't think she reads the Bible much either, but she listens in church and picks up on its explanations.

I see the Bible as like an extension of Greek mythology. The stories are pretty good, and ideas like love and forgiveness are important to talk about. Like Smith's abstractions, they guide our lives. If everyone lived like Jesus said we should, the world would be a better place. But we don't do that. The people at church are pretty hypocritical and tend to be kind of narrow-minded. They use what they read in the Bible selectively, to support what they want to think instead of opening up and using it to try to become wise.

Using the idea of this loving God guy or Jesus guy to tell you what to do, or keep the loneliness away, is sure tempting. When I first started cutting myself, I used to try to pray, but it just made me feel worse, lonelier than ever, because when I prayed, nothing happened, absolutely nothing, and I was being sincere. I mean when I go to the beach, which I was doing here quite often before Grant, and when I look out over the water at the mountains on the other side, or just sit on a log and watch the waves, something happens. I actually start to feel happy. I feel soothed and it doesn't matter as much that I feel alone, because nature makes sense even if it is indifferent to individuals. Bonnie and Sterling's church had the opposite effect. It just made me feel more alone.

Okay, about the cutting. People don't seem to get it and they get all weird about it, but it seems obvious to me. You may be wondering about it. I'll try to explain. It's for the same reason people become anorexic or bulimic or alcoholics or sports fans, or watch tragic plays for that matter. It makes them feel better!

The first time I did it, years ago, I was in my room, and already feeling depressed, when these boys called. Bonnie was watching TV and Sterling was on the phone in the other room, talking real estate. I was doing my homework, which has always been a way of escaping from them. I don't dread it the way some kids do, because I actually like reading and learning new things. But sometimes it doesn't engage me enough to pull me away into a place where I can feel more excited about life. Although lately, as I've gotten older, my homework has been part of the problem. It makes me think about things too much.

That night I was working on a science project, a poster on tornados that I liked doing, but Sterling's voice kept getting loud, which broke into my thoughts and annoyed me and made me think about a story I was reading called The Education of Little Tree. It's about this Indian kid who lives in the mountains with his grandparents. Even though they're poor and white people don't treat them well, it's obvious they love each other. Comparing it to my life made me feel trapped, alone and totally invisible.

I was in eighth grade and starting to develop, but I was still skinny and too tall, and really self-conscious. When my cell rang, I thought it would be someone calling to ask about a homework assignment, but it wasn't. The person talking tried to disguise his voice to make it all low and gravelly, but I could hear giggling in the background, so I knew it was a kid and he wasn't alone. Anyway, he said my name and that he wanted to (blank) me and some other stuff about my long, skinny legs and my nipples. It was gross, and the stupid part was that my phone had caller ID so I knew where the call came from. The kid went to my church.

I hung up and he tried to call back, but I turned the phone off. I didn't know Natalie yet or I would have called her. Crying might have helped, but I don't do much of that either. It's a lot like praying. It's only good if you think someone who cares hears you. I was trimming some construction paper with one of those razor knives that artists use. I was making frames for the tornado pictures I was going to glue onto the poster board. I started by poking the knife point into the back of my left forearm, maybe because I wanted to stab those boys, or maybe because I was mad at myself after finding out that I was someone guys thought of that way.

I wasn't really thinking that specifically. I just know that the pain in my arm made me quit thinking about what they said, and that it was a better kind of pain because it was easier to understand. So I decided to see if I was strong enough to actually cut the skin and draw blood. I did it on my upper arm so I could cover it with my sleeve. It was hard to make my hand do it, but I was able to, and it softened the awful feeling I had from getting the phone call on top of feeling low and empty already. Maybe it's the blood. I usually wipe it with my finger and lick it.

Until I came here, I was still doing it. I never told Natalie and I didn't do it that much. I saved it for the big stuff. Like I did it after I found the birth certificate. I'm lucky because I have dark skin and scars don't show, especially fine razor scars. As soon as I get a little tan on them, they're pretty much gone, so I usually cut my thighs high enough above my knees that they're always covered and I go to the tanning booth at Bonnie's fitness center once in a while and no one knows.

I've wondered a lot about my life with Bonnie before Sterling, and who my real father is and if he's alive, but I didn't consciously come here looking for him. In fact, I didn't know I was thinking about him until it came out of my mouth when the customs guy asked why I was coming to Canada. So maybe this is all about me figuring out where the warmth will come from, and because I'm almost an adult and it's time to make decisions about college and real life, something big had to happen now for the next step to make sense.

Bonnie's my mom, but I don't feel close to her at all. Not much warmth there. Even though I can't say I've been miserable, for most of my life, just playing along sure hasn't made me happy. It's true that I wasn't hungry. I wasn't cold or in great physical pain. I didn't mind school. Sports were okay. People didn't tease me or single me out in a bad way very often. (When I heard that those same boys who called me in eighth grade had called several other girls, it made me feel better.) But in the last few years, it's like I've started thinking too much, and that's made the emptiness grow way too big, and I've been finding myself in this cold, dark, hopeless place with no way out.

I had to do something.

Corey

It's the same room where I saw my parents. The puke green paint is so old you can see how it faded where the light coming through the wire covering the little window hits it. There is, of course, the camera mounted from the ceiling, not as corny as a one-way mirror, but still annoying. There's nothing else but a beat-up old table with a scuffed-up, cheapo plastic top, and two battered wooden chairs.

Smith is already sitting in one of the chairs. He's wearing his usual khaki pants and a dark polo. His hair is graying but still has streaks of brown and is combed back—kind of wavy, old guy hair, not too long, but not the way a kid would ever wear it. It suits him though. He stands and shakes my hand. He doesn't usually strike you as an old guy. His eyes are really alive, but today, even through his glasses, they look tired.

"Hi, Corey."

I look down, clear my throat and say,

"Mr. Smith."

"They're not too big on warmth here, are they?" he says.

"Nope." I still don't look up.

"How's the food?"

"Not good. Not bad. Like school food."

"Okay, Corey," he says. "I don't like small talk, and I didn't come here to talk about the food or the dreariness of the place. I'm sure being here is pretty miserable, probably a lot like doing chemo in the hospital. I'll just say it. You know how I've been fighting cancer and have been in remission. I've talked about it in class. Well, last week I went to the doctor for my cancer check and got bad results. Nothing's certain yet, but it seems to be coming back. I drove by this place on the way home and thought about you in here, and I realized we have something in common."

I don't want to hear this, not on top of everything else. I mean, Shit! Sometimes life just fucking sucks. I clear my throat and try to think of something to say, but nothing comes and I'm glad when he starts talking again.

"There are lots of ways of being trapped. You probably understand better than most people what I'm feeling now, and sometimes it helps just to know someone else is struggling with a similar situation. Maybe we can help each other. Having no control over your fate can feel pretty lonely."

"Yeah, I guess I know about that." I try to imagine having cancer and can't, except I think, for me, it might be a relief, a convenient way to check out.

"Maybe I'm here to say that good things sometimes come from bad situations and, at least from one person's point of view, it's worth it to hang on. Maybe I need to say it to you so I can believe it myself, because sometimes I think it would be easier to let go of hope and get it over with. Sometimes the uncertainty feels worse than just accepting my fate and letting go."

Yeah, I know about wanting to let go. If I had cancer, I wouldn't have to imagine hanging myself from the sprinklers anymore. What the hell good can come from even your mother believing you did something awful? Jesus, Smith, at least you have a life, something you actually want to hold onto.

"Life is a crazy business, Corey, and you've drawn a tough hand to play. Maybe I'm just here to let you know I know that, and to tell you that my life is a little rough now too. I keep getting extensions, reprieves, and I haven't let go yet, and I'm glad I haven't, because a lot of good things have happened to me too since I first got sick. Teaching has been good for me. It's changed

my life and I wouldn't want to go back to being the person I was
before, but I also wouldn't wish the cancer experience on my
worst enemy."

I'm still speechless. I mean what can I say?

"I told the detective after Kristen disappeared that I didn't
think you could have hurt her and that I thought you were friends,
but he didn't seem very interested. So I don't think I can help
your case much. From what I hear and read in the papers, they
don't have much evidence, even though they seem convinced
you're guilty. What will you do if they let you out?"

"I don't know. Probably stay at my dad's." Wait a minute. You
actually told the detective you didn't think I did it?

"When I was first diagnosed I would daydream that the
cancer would just go away and that I would go to the doctor and
they would tell me it was all a mistake and they had mixed up
the lab samples, even though it was clear that my body was really
sick. I just didn't want what was happening to me to be true. I'll
bet you find yourself hoping that Kristen is safe somewhere and
just ran off, and that she'll show up wondering what all the fuss
is about."

Harold has a saying for this. "Wish in one hand, shit in the
other. See which one fills up first." What I say to Smith is, "Fat
chance."

"That's what I would have said when I was first diagnosed if
someone had predicted I would still be here ten years later, talking
to you, but here I am. Strange things do happen. But you're right.
It seems pretty unlikely. By now she would have found a way to
contact Natalie or her parents, or you. But it won't stay a mystery
forever. Eventually something will surface. Someone will know
something. She didn't just evaporate from her car at the mall."

"Mr. Smith, this is really important, so don't lie to me, okay."

He meets my eyes. "Corey, I didn't come here to lie."

"You didn't come here to trick me into confessing?"

"No."

"Did you really tell the detective you didn't think I did it?"

"Yes."

"Do you still believe that?"

"Yes."

"Why?"

"I don't know. A feeling. I follow my instincts. They're accurate most of the time. Not always. My take on you is that the adults in your life haven't lived up to your expectations, and you've got some things to work out about authority and finding a direction and a way to connect with people. I watched you and Kristen together. You were connecting. She saw the same good things in you that I see, and I don't think you could harm her intentionally, even if she did something that hurt you.

"I don't think either of you would harm the other intentionally, but people tend to protect themselves at the expense of others, and we often don't think through the consequences of what we do. I can't imagine you causing her death in any way but an accident or a moment of rage. We all have emotional hot buttons, but if that had happened, I don't think you would have tried to conceal what you did. You'd have told them right away, because that would be far easier than what you're going through now. You may be angry because your life feels crappy, but the truth matters to you, and I think you would step up and take responsibility the way you wish adults would. It really is just a feeling. I could be wrong. Am I?"

"No." I looked directly into his eyes, no faltering, and said, "I miss her. She understood being alone the same way I do, and she trusted me. People don't trust me much, but she did. Do you really think she might be alive?"

"It's a nice thought, Corey, and I held on to it as long as I could, but now..."

"I told her a story about my uncle running away when he was

our age, and I like to imagine that she did it."

"It would certainly surprise a lot of people."

After he left, I tried to imagine Kristen turning up alive, but I couldn't. I was letting go of that hope like Smith did about his cancer going away. I thought I should be sad because of his bad news about it, and I was glad he did most of the talking because it helped cover up my not knowing what to say. The news that he believed me made it hard for me to concentrate on what he might be feeling.

Kristen

After I got a motel room that first day, I just went with the vacation feeling. I mean, why not? Corey's story about his uncle was my inspiration. This isn't Hawaii, but the day I arrived, the weather was pretty nice. Even though there are rainy days, it hasn't been bad. The city is beautiful, and just looking at the buildings and the greenery puts me in a good mood. Until I got the job, I worried about money. I knew I wouldn't last long living like a homeless person. This whole thing, my being here, has been a pretty amazing story. No wonder I got suckered by Grant.

I had to stay at a motel for only a week. Now I share this house with Ian and Char. They're not a couple. They don't share a room or sleep together, but it seems like they've been friends forever. He seems safe and sometimes I wonder if maybe, even if he isn't sure about it himself, he's gay. They went to the same high school together and have a lot of inside jokes. They're both nice and like I said, they don't seem dangerous or anything, and I don't worry about my stuff being stolen. I don't have much to steal anyway, so what I really mean is they respect my space and my room feels private.

The house belongs to Ian's uncle who plans to remodel it and move into it himself, but he isn't ready to start yet, so he's letting Ian rent it cheap. Most of the houses around here have already been fixed up, so the neighborhood doesn't have the ghetto feel that it would if they were all still like this one. We let it get pretty messy and, like Natalie, Ian and Char smoke. Mainly, they don't bother me and I can afford my share of the rent.

Ian and Char are from Port Alberni, a mill town on the west side of Vancouver Island. Coming to Victoria was also a pretty big adventure for them, and it couldn't have happened if Ian's uncle hadn't had this house available. They both graduated last year and seem to be taking a break after high school, trying out working and living away from their parents. They came the same week I got here, which had something to do with how we met.

They wanted to go to Vancouver, but their parents talked them out of it. I'm glad, because I think Vancouver is more dangerous and because I'm getting to share their good fortune. The house was really kind of a gift by the uncle to help guide their decision. They had enough money saved to pay rent for the first month, but they needed jobs and another person to contribute rent money if they wanted to stay. They found jobs in shops that sell stuff to tourists, and they found me to help with the rent.

When I came here in April, the streets were already crawling with tourists. That first day, after lying on the motel bed for a while, letting my new situation settle in, and all wired with the improbability of being here, I went looking for cheap food. I figured that by eating cheap, I could use a little money for fun. I hadn't eaten since Anacortes and I found the perfect restaurant. My lucky streak began.

It's the kind of place you'd walk past unless you were looking for an inexpensive meal. There are windows that look out on the sidewalk, but the front of the building is drab and the sign on the window closest to the door is faded. It's a few blocks up the hill from the harbor, on a side street. I was hungry and wanted a place to sit that didn't have that cheesy, fake-upbeat feel that fast food restaurants have and that end up being depressing. It was early afternoon by then, but there were still a lot of people eating, so I went in.

That's when I met Trudy, and how I got my job. Pretty

unbelievable! She doesn't look like Trish, Natalie's aunt, at all, but she has some of the same mannerisms. She showed me to a table and took my order for a club sandwich. She brought milk with my tea. I'd never had it that way before. Mainly what I've learned about her is that her inner person, the part that our poet friend, Emily, would call the soul, seems familiar in a good, warm way and it's right out there on the surface for me to see, which is amazing, considering how I've lived with Bonnie forever and don't feel at all that way about her.

Of course I didn't figure all this out that first day. That first day, it was just a kind of nice feeling I got from her. She made me feel welcome and it helped me stay in my vacation mode and not lapse into feeling alone and lost in a strange city. The third time I ate there it was later in the afternoon and Trudy wasn't very busy, so we struck up a conversation.

I think she was pretty once, and her hair was probably dark brown when she was younger. It's so mixed with gray now, it's hard to tell. She has kids who are grown and don't live around here, and I can tell she misses them. She's had kind of a hard life and never had much money. She smokes, too. It's made her skin wrinkly and she looks older than she is. She asked if I was here on vacation and I told the same lie I told the customs guy about coming to see my father, but I expanded it, mixing it with some truth, and said that I had never met my dad but that I knew he lived in the Victoria area and I was going to try to find him. I told her I was from Seattle.

After about a week or so of eating there every day, she told me the restaurant owner was looking for a temporary waitress because one of the other women wanted a few months off to help her daughter take care of a new grandchild. She said the daughter had had complications with the delivery, had other small children, and was still pretty sick. If I was going to be around for a while it might help me stretch my money, and I would be doing someone a big favor at the same time. By then I had already met Ian and Char and was staying here. I had given Ian a month's rent even though I wasn't sure I could stretch my money that long, but moving in with them was an easy choice because ten days in the motel cost more than what Ian needed for a month. The job offer was too perfect, like an answered prayer. It made it easy to avoid the thought of going back.

Meeting Ian and Char was another piece of luck that I can only attribute to fate. It was the first night, and for the first time in my life, I could just walk into a bar if I wanted. I chose one, picked a table and ordered fish and chips and pear cider. The waitress didn't even ask for my ID. There was a hockey game on the big screen TV. The couple at the next table were really getting into it, and when the guy—his name turned out to be Ian—went off to the bathroom, the girl, Char, asked me which team I was for. I didn't have an answer because I don't know much about hockey except that it's a lot like soccer, only on ice.

We talked a little that night. They asked if I lived here. Since they were new in town, they were trying to meet people and get connected. The town they came from sounded small, like Mount Vernon, and it's pretty isolated, so they knew a lot of people there and were used to people being friendly. I told them the same story I told Trudy, that I was trying to connect with my dad and that I didn't know how long I'd stay. After that night, we kept running into each other, and they kind of adopted me and offered to let me share the house.

Actually getting hired had to be guided by fate at least as much as finding a place to stay. I was worried about not having the Canadian version of a social security number, called a Social Insurance Number (SIN for short; I think that's funny). Char told me it would be easy to get one since I have my birth certificate, but sending in an official application for a government document scared me. So far, nothing I'd done here had been very visible, and when I went into the back office at the restaurant to talk to Mr. Wickam—his first name is Leigh, like Lee only with British spelling—I didn't have one.

I was expecting to meet this adult man, which I guess he is, but he's only in his twenties, and after I talked to him and had the job, Trudy told me his father has money and owns the building and the restaurant too. Leigh dropped out of college and is the black sheep in the family, but needs their money, so he's running the restaurant until his dad figures out what he wants to do with it. Trudy thinks the father is testing him and says that Leigh's not a bad guy to work for. Since he doesn't really know what he's doing, he listens to the employees and because of that, no one has really cheated him yet.

He was checking me out during the interview, flirting, which made me uncomfortable. He has a slight British accent and some people would think he's good-looking, but he makes me nervous. He's not my type, but I'm glad for the job and probably won't have to be around him much. He said that since I was temporary and would likely go back to the States anyway, he would just pay me cash, under the table. If a card became necessary, we could deal with it then.

Natalie

Brad is real conscientious and knows what he's doing. I watched him put the boat away, and when he was done, everything was exactly as it was when we got there. I pay attention to things like that, like whether people are flaky or not, because I don't trust flaky people. I asked him if he was being so careful because he wasn't supposed to use the boat and we were getting away with it because his parents weren't home. I think I hurt his feelings, but that's the kind of relationship we have because of how we met. I get to say what I think. He's not flaky. Like when we were in the boat, you could tell he knew what he was doing, and he was careful to explain safety things. Most kids don't do that kind of thing, but he has this earnestness about him, like he wants to do right and if someone will show him how, he'll do it, even if it's hard. Maybe that's why we get along.

So the boat was put away and we were in his rooms. He doesn't just have a room; it's like an apartment. It was around dinnertime, and we were hungry because we didn't take anything to eat on the boat with us. I was in the shower when his mother came home, which of course may not have looked so good to her in spite of what we know about the wrestling coach affair, and Brad was in the kitchen, making corned-beef-and-Swiss-cheese sandwiches. He had planned ahead and went to Haggens' yesterday, which I thought was nice. So she came down to let him know she was home and heard the shower running which, so far, only meant that he had a friend with him.

Since I took my backpack with fresh clothes into the bathroom with me, she didn't know I wasn't a guy. Brad and I haven't done anything yet, so it was only natural that I'd want privacy to dress. We've only come close to what you'd call making out twice, and it's kind of tender and careful when we do even that much. It feels a little dangerous because friendships get wrecked by that stuff, and neither of us is sure what kind of relationship we have. I'm normally not shy about my body, because I'm of proud of it. I think I look good in a bathing suit, and it was okay being with Brad and wearing one all day, but I'm still cautious around him. I care what he thinks. I think suggestive clothes make you think about sex as much as being naked does, so I wasn't about to parade around in a towel. When I came out, I was fully dressed, but my maroon hair was still wet.

I was combing it in front of this big mirror that's on the back wall of the bar and kitchen area. I have several piercings in my ears, not just the lobes, but up toward the top too, and with the light playing off my wet hair, the silver really stood out. I asked Brad if I could borrow his hair dryer. From the bathroom, I hadn't heard a thing when she came down the first time, so she startled me by coming down the stairs behind me.

She was still dressed from the day and she's quite good-looking, like she might have competed in beauty pageants when she was younger. She was manicured, not just in the carefully groomed sense, but her nails too, fingers and toes. She is what you'd call willowy, thin but not skinny, like rich girls you see in movies playing tennis, healthy and evenly tanned. She was wearing a tailored silk top and Capris, with the kind of leather sandals you see at Nordstrom's that cost more than I make in three months, and tasteful jewelry that Kristen's mom would like to wear and tries to imitate.

And there I am just out of her son's shower, nice body, wearing this Old Navy stuff I got on sale with lots of cheapo silver on my ears and a fake diamond in my nose, combing my maroon hair. At least I don't have a tattoo yet. I'm putting it off until I'm eighteen. She smiled icicles at me.

"Introduce me to your friend, Bradley," she said with that professional politeness the snooty girls at the make-up counter in Macy's use.

"This is Natalie. Natalie, this is Jean Stanfield, my mom."

I was proud of him. You could feel the tension between them, but he didn't cower or let her make me feel small.

I said, "It's nice to meet you, Mrs. Stanfield."

I met her eyes for a brief moment and felt the assumption behind them that she would never stoop to say out loud. She thought Brad had brought me home to get even with her by having sex with a trampy girl, using me to soil her already fouled house.

I looked her in the eye and said, "Brad and I spent the afternoon on the lake. He said you grew up here, in the other house. It's very beautiful. You're awfully lucky."

More icicles and the dismissal, "It's nice you got a chance to enjoy it, Natalie. Bradley, don't forget that your grandparents are coming home tonight. I know you'll want to be here, so you should take your friend home early. The Jensens are coming for lunch tomorrow. They're coming early and Lauren will be with them. She's dying to see you."

With that, she was up the stairs and we were alone again.

"I didn't lie, did I?" Brad said.

"What do you mean?"

"I told you I was the son of a bitch. And now you've met her. My grandparents are actually nice."

Of course I wanted to ask about Lauren, but I didn't. I was surprised at the way Brad just tuned his mother out after she left. We took our time eating the sandwiches, then watched a movie and hung out for a while before he took me home. That was last night. It might have been too late to see his grandparents when he got home, but I'm pretty sure that when he calls he'll tell me about his day, probably answering my curiosity about Lauren.

I wonder if he and his mom got along before he walked in on her, and if she's been having affairs all along, but this is the first time she got caught, or if it's something new that just happened and she's having to adjust, figure out how to make her world keep working. Everyone has a story. Now, because of Brad, she's in my life too, but in spite of her, it was still a pretty nice day.

Kristen

After Grant dropped me off that day I met him, I leaned the bike against the side of the house, not bothering to lock it, and went in. The only reason I remembered his name is because his last name is Mackenzie, the same as my real father's. He was very polite when I got in the car and he introduced himself, like he understood that I might be a little wary. I ended up telling him my name too, the one I go by here, Amy Mackenzie, mainly because it took me by surprise that his last name is the same. It still feels good to be rid of the name connection to Sterling.

For the rest of the day, I took a lot of Ibuprophen, read, iced my ankle, and pretty much just vegged out. The ice packs helped, and even though my foot was still pretty sore, I managed to work a short shift the next day. One of Char's friends gave me a ride to work. I would have gone home on the bus, but Leigh gave me a ride to save me from having to walk the several blocks from the bus stop to my house. It's hard to think of Leigh as my boss or as Mr. Wickam. He acts young and I've even seen him out with his friends a few times at some of the bars we go to.

It's not that far from the restaurant to the house, but the traffic was heavy and we were stuck long enough so that Leigh felt the need to make conversation. He asked how I hurt my ankle. I thought he was just being polite, but I told him what happened because it gave me something to say. It turns out he rides a mountain bike and knows a good bike shop. He didn't think it would cost much to replace the chain, but the bike would have to

go to the shop. He offered to drop it off there for me on his way
back to the restaurant. I could pick it up later and ride it home.
He even had a bike rack on his car, so I was feeling pretty happy.
My problem was solved. Until we pulled up in front of the house.

The bike was gone.

We looked around the side and in the back yard in case Ian
or Char had moved it. We even looked in the garage, which is
full of Ian's uncle's stuff. I was pretty sure it wouldn't be there
and it wasn't. It was a little weird bringing Leigh into the house,
which was even messier than usual, but, like me, he had a hard
time believing the bike had been stolen, and it became our project
to look together. I apologized for the messy house because he is
my boss and I work in a restaurant, so cleanliness does matter. I
didn't want him to think I'm a slob. The experience broadened
my view of him. He was nice, not like some spoiled rich kid, and
he's not bad-looking either.

That evening I was watching TV alone when Grant showed up.
We don't have cable, so there's not much on. I had finished my
book and was trying to stay off my foot, and I was watching
a news program about the war in Iraq. It all seems like such a
mess where everyone is going to lose. You'd think if the Iraqis
could talk to each other without everyone being so stubborn, they
wouldn't have to kill each other.

I was really startled when I opened the door. I mean Grant
was the last person I expected to see. He was dressed casually,
but again, quality stuff, a really nice polo, chinos and loafers.
He's younger than Sterling, but seems more like that generation
and dresses that way. Just off the porch behind him, the bike was
standing upright on the kickstand. I noticed immediately that the
chain had been fixed.

He gestured toward it. "Good as new," he said.

At first I was speechless.

"I wanted to surprise you," he said.

"I don't know what to say," was what came out. It wasn't the happy kind of surprise he was looking for. "I thought it was stolen. It surprised me that anyone would want it. Now I'm even more surprised."

"I'm sorry I worried you. I was afraid that if I waited until you returned, you might not let me do it. You seem very independent. I hope you'll forgive me and indulge me this. It's been quite fun, actually."

I thought of Leigh's offer to get it fixed, and how his concern made me like him more, and how maybe if you're a guy, it's fun to help a damsel in distress. But this gave me one of those wary feelings. I'm not good at speaking my mind, so I thought about what Natalie would do in this situation, and I said what I thought she might say.

"So why? Why me? Do you go around getting people's stuff fixed? I can take care of myself. I'm not some starving, stray dog. I came home from work earlier with a friend to pick up the bike to get it fixed. I though it had been stolen. So yeah, I was upset."

"I'm sorry. You are absolutely right. I should have waited and asked."

"You could have left a note."

He looked hurt and it made me feel bad; maybe he did just want to be helpful and make the world a better place. I had presented him with an opportunity and he had taken advantage of it. Now I was being a jerk.

"Look, it was a really nice thing to do," I said. "And people usually don't go around being nice. When it was gone I got upset, but that's no reason to be rude. I apologize. Thank you. You're a nice man and you did a very thoughtful thing."

He smiled. "No. You're right. I was out of line. I'm the one who should apologize. I was being selfish and thoughtless, but I really do take pleasure in smoothing out life's little bumps. On my way home after dropping you off, I noticed a bike repair shop, and then earlier today I was in your neighborhood. It was very spur-of-the-moment. I knocked on the door to tell you, but you weren't home. Fixing your bike seemed like such an easy way to make someone happy, but I messed it up."

"It was just a communication problem. It's not the end of the world."

"Can we be friends anyway?" He held out his hand.

"Friends," I said. I shook his hand. "And now I don't have to take the bus tomorrow. Thanks, friend."

As he was opening his car door to leave, he turned and said, "Are you hungry? Can a friend buy a friend a bite to eat?"

I hadn't had anything but a few Doritos and a banana since I left the restaurant that afternoon. I was hungry and it seemed harmless enough. After all, we had the same last name. He could even be my uncle.

Kristen

So Grant took me to dinner. We went to this little town called Brentwood Bay. It's on the Saanich Inlet. It took about half an hour to get there and I could have said no, but I didn't. Here's how it happened. I got in the car. Remember, it's a Cadillac and quite nice, but it's not like I haven't ridden in nice cars before. Sterling drives a Mercedes. We were heading towards town, like he had a particular place in mind, when he looked over and said, "Do you need to be back right away?"

"I have to work tomorrow, but I don't have to open up or do breakfast. I'm good for a while."

"We live in a beautiful city. I'm sure you know that already, but there are some places outside the city that are quite wonderful." He looked at his watch. "We still have enough daylight. I know the perfect place to eat, but it's a bit of a drive. It will be worth it. Do you mind?"

I wasn't totally comfortable with the idea, so I said, "I'm not dressed for a nice restaurant."

"You look fine," he said. "If we always bend to society's rules, we miss half the joy in life."

So I agreed to go.

We headed out of town toward the ferry dock. He asked me if I had been to Butchart Gardens, and when I said I hadn't, he promised to take me. He said that when the roses were in bloom it was truly glorious. I noticed the word, "glorious," because it's not a word people in the Valley often use. He was like a tour guide and a salesman at the same time, very enthusiastic, and it made me wonder if he sold real estate, like Sterling.

Listening to him made me get over my nervousness about going with him. He was very polite and thoughtful, and his talk was interesting. When we got there, the restaurant had a great view of the inlet. Since it was a weeknight and a little late for dinner, it was pretty low-key inside. I could tell when we drove up that it would be expensive, so, thinking like Natalie, I said,

"For a friend buying a friend a bite to eat, this is pretty upscale. When it's my turn, I'll feel inadequate. "

"This is you doing me a favor," he said. "Don't let it make you uncomfortable. I like good food and a nice view. My life has been good to me and I can afford them. I enjoy being with my friends. You're my friend. I'll tell you up front, I don't expect you to reciprocate. You've forgiven me for my thoughtlessness today and you're sharing your time. So humor me and please let me do this for you."

So I did.

Sterling and Bonnie like expensive restaurants, and I've had plenty of experience with them, which means the restaurant wasn't intimidating. I was comparing Grant to Sterling in the same situation. Sterling can be pushy and is often rude to the waiters. Grant was very polite.

He ordered a bottle of wine, Pinot Gris from Oregon, just for me, because he ate a steak and even I know that you're supposed to drink red wine with steak. The crab-dip hors d'oeuvres were amazing. I ordered halibut for my entree. It was fresh, with this lemon sauce that was a specialty of the restaurant. Everything was wonderful. Remember, I'd been eating most of my meals at Leigh's restaurant and it's not bad, but it's heavy and greasy and a little on the boring side. Since I haven't had a lot of drinking experience, I just sipped the wine.

As we ate, Grant asked the kind of questions you would ask when you're trying to get to know someone. I didn't feel like he was prying. He wanted to know if I grew up in Victoria, that kind of thing. I won't bore you by trying to recreate the conversation. Considering my situation as a fugitive runaway, it would have been perfectly reasonable for me to stay in character as Amy and tell the story I'd been telling about being born in Canada but growing up in Seattle and coming here to settle something about my origin. After all, my birth certificate says I really am Amy.

Instead I told him this story about growing up in California. Sterling has family in California and we've visited them. I said I went to Redwood High School because one of my fake cousins, Sterling's nephew, went there, and a long time ago Robin Williams went there too, so at least I knew it was a real place. I was vague about specifics, but Grant didn't press me. He really is a master at making you feel comfortable.

If you think about it, and I have had to lately, there are lots of little stories you can tell about yourself that aren't specific to a place. I mean schools are pretty much the same everywhere, and situations between people aren't much different either, so I've been learning to filter everything I say so that it could have happened in Seattle or California instead of the Valley. Once you get the hang of it, it's not that hard.

Fate had brought me this far. And if I really wanted to know the truth about myself, he might have been the perfect connection. For all I knew, he could really be my uncle or cousin or something. Or he could have some government job where he might be able to find the answers to the questions I have about my roots.

He has traveled all over the world and knows about food and wine and puts a lot of importance on the atmosphere of a place, like how the food, the wine, the smells, the view and feel of a place go together to set up a perfect mood. He's a good storyteller and can make you see what he's describing. He puts you under this intimate spell, so there weren't any uncomfortably quiet moments, in spite of the fact that I didn't have much to say. The wine was good with the halibut, and looking out through the fading light at this beautiful tree-lined fjord, I sipped it while I listened.

I couldn't help but think about how that particular moment, finding myself—whoever I am, Kristen Nichols and/or Amy Mackenzie—in that restaurant with that particular man, was the result of so many other unlikely moments that maybe I should at least have told him Amy's story. Maybe I should have given him that much and let him help me find out who I really am, if he could. Maybe it was my big chance. But my instinct was totally against it. It didn't feel right to tell him about wanting to find my father.

Amy lied. Kristen double-lied. I'm not sure why I did it, but it turned out to be a good call.

It was a pleasant evening, and Grant was good to his word. He got me home early so it wasn't hard to get up for work the next day. The new chain on the bicycle got me there and riding gave me time to think on the way. I would have to explain to Leigh and Trudy about getting the bike back. If I told them the truth about Grant being this random, older guy from the park and about dinner last night, it would sound strange, and they would worry. So I fibbed a little and used our having the same last name to imply that he was a relative and part of my trying to connect with my family here.

On my way to work, I passed those big government buildings that must be full of records about people from all over British Columbia. I knew my father's name, and if I had really wanted to, I could've started looking. But I had the feeling that once I made that move, I'd end up going back, and I wasn't ready.

Corey

The detective who's assigned to me and whose personal mission is to put me away came to tell me he'll be watching every move I make after I get out because he knows I did it and that eventually I will make a mistake.

When Smith was here to see me, he said up front that he didn't come because he thought he could help me, but because he thought we had something in common, like he needed a friend too, and I might understand his situation better than other people. His believing in me and putting it that way allowed me to speak out to the cop a little more, to say things I might not have said before. So when the jerk said he would find a way to nail me, I said, "I'm innocent. How're you going to feel when you find out it's true?"

"You're not."

"But I am, and someday someone will come forward, or the right piece of evidence will be found."

"You're going to fry."

"You'll look like a fool."

Then after I got him to admit that my English teacher said he believes me, the bastard had to add that some people can't face unpleasant truths, as though Smith was some kind of weakling.

I'm out of there.

They had to let me go, and on getaway day, when it finally quit raining and the clouds broke, it was good to feel the sun warm my face again. It wasn't the pure joy-of-release kind of time a person might fantasize about, but a day of complex emotions.

Smith messes me up. He's probably the only one who believes me, and especially since he went out of his way to say so, his believing makes it harder than if I was completely alone. He said it can be more painful to try to live right than it would be to just let go and give up, and his believing in me kind of hangs there behind me when I'm feeling sorry for myself. It complicates things.

It didn't stop me from getting into my dad's vodka as soon as I could, but it was floating around in my thoughts, spoiling the purity of the plunge I was trying to take. My dad only took the morning off to come get me. I'm sure just having people know I'm his son is bad enough, especially on top of the fact of his already marginal, alcoholic life. I had to blow the breathalyzer thing in his car to start it so we could get out of the courthouse parking lot. Then I had to do it again when he left the house to go to work.

This was a bad day for him. Most of the time he doesn't act sloppy drunk and you wouldn't see it right away if you didn't know him. He usually regulates himself during the day to get through work. But once he's home in the evening, he moves it to another level. He slurs and forgets things. He watches a lot of TV and he sleeps a lot, so at least he's not in my face making me feel like a worm, the way Harold would be if I'd had to go to my mom's house.

If Smith hadn't stopped by Juvie, and if I didn't know that there was at least one rational, respectable person in the world that saw me as something different than a sex-pervert psycho killer, it would have been a lot easier to follow my dad's example and pickle myself into oblivion. As it was, I did a pretty good job of it anyway, but it wasn't clean. By the time the sun came out, I was lying on a dirty blanket amidst the clutter of my dad's back yard, letting the rays warm me. I had a pretty good buzz going. I was drinking it straight, like the old man does. I was trying to let go, to be in the moment, to wash everything but the warmth of the sun away. But I was thinking about Smith, and the idea of him knowing I was turning into my father was humiliating. The numbness wasn't entirely comfortable.

So I tried to write Smith off by imagining things like maybe he is one of those guys who likes young boys and was trying to set me up so he could seduce me. It didn't work because I have instincts, and when I pay attention, I can tell about people. Smith wasn't lying. He's just stuck with an inconvenient belief that involves me. Everyone has inconvenient beliefs. Most people ignore them when they can, and become kind of hypocritical. They put things off and try to stay numb. Because he might be dying, Smith has less to lose by being honest. I mean if he's going to check out pretty quick, what does he care if people think he's some kind of bleeding heart that can't face it that one of his students is a killer. If he actually believes it, he's stuck with it, just like I'm stuck with it.

The truth does matter.

And my truth is that it's better to be out and staying at my dad's house in Burlington than to be back inside or staying with my mom and Harold. But it's not so good here. I'm still trapped by my situation. I'm just penned up in a different way, in a different place. I don't feel as safe. I feel like if I go to the mall or just become visible to the wrong people, I'll get beat up, or worse. People get beat up and even killed just for being gay or black.

My getting out was in the paper. Even though there was no picture, it was a front-page story right alongside a story about some kid from Mount Vernon getting blown up by a suicide bomber in Afghanistan. Sometimes at night when I hear car doors slam outside and men talking, I worry that someone will throw a gasoline bomb into the house or break in to do what the law couldn't. I think I understand what Smith's life is like, knowing the end is coming, but not being sure and not knowing when. It's easy to wish it would just happen and get it over with.

I have this fantasy about going to the school and being out in front when they break for lunch and everyone is heading across the street to the cafeteria. I would stand at the bottom of the stairs at the main entrance and yell, "All right you fuckers, I miss her too. I'm back, and I didn't do it. You don't believe me and I hate you all, so come on. Just do whatever you've got to do to make your fucking world feel right-side up again."

Sometimes it ends with them coming at me, swarming me, killing me. Sometimes I have a bomb strapped to myself. Sometimes I have an assault rifle. They're just fantasies, the same as dreaming of having a bomb strapped under my shirt to scare Harold or the principal was before all this. I still don't think I can do it. The news is so full of that kind of thing. It seems to be getting worse all the time. I mean, all over the world, people are at that crazy, blurry place where you just pop. So it's not like I'm the only one who feels that way. Like Smith says, there are lots of ways to be trapped.

None of my old friends have called. They won't. Or, if they do, it won't be out of friendship, but out of curiosity, to be the one who actually talked to the killer. I didn't have any really close friends, the kind that stick with you, like Natalie was to Kristen. I don't think I'd call someone that I thought was a pervert.

I stole some money from the old man and was able to score some weed. I got it from this Mexican kid I know in Mount Vernon. He was in Texas when Kristen disappeared. If he knew about me, he didn't say anything, but I was still really nervous about getting beat up, so I had him meet me at one of those gas stations on Old 99. He pulled up with a car full of guys, which scared me, but nobody said anything and nothing happened. I gave him the money. He gave me the baggy, and they drove off. Maybe I'm paranoid.

My dad's house is in the crummy part of Burlington, east of

the tracks and south of what used to be the town before all the malls went in on Old 99. They talked about getting me enrolled at the high school here to finish the year, but since there are only a few days of school left, the teacher lady from Juvie said she would keep working with me to get the assignments done from my old school and turn in my work there.

If I could go away, I would. I fantasize about disappearing to Mexico more than ever now. I could just disappear, like Kristen did. Maybe I'd end up dead, and maybe I wouldn't. I don't have any money and don't speak Spanish. Maybe, if I really wanted to, I could pull it off, but I'd have to steal first. I could just take off hitching, or get a bus ticket to some place far away. I'm not eighteen and without ID that says I am, it would be hard to find a job.

But if I run I look guilty for sure. There's a court date coming up from the drug charge and if I miss it, I'm in more trouble. For now, I'm just waiting until I can't take it anymore, or someone finds out what really happened. The best thing would be to go live with someone who didn't think I was a criminal, someone far away where I could go to stores, walk around in public, get a job, go to school. But no one wants me. No one wants to be associated with me, not even my sister. Staying with her in Seattle would be way better than being here, only she doesn't have room and it would complicate her life. We're not that close, I mean, for me to ask her to make sacrifices.

I try to pass the time. Sometimes I use school work as a distraction, just like when I was inside, and I still have my imagination. I read some and watch a lot of TV, and when nothing else works, I either get high on the old man's vodka or I smoke a little. At night I walk.

The worst thing about being let out was totally unexpected. Juvie has this strange feel, like it's on a different planet or exists in a dream. Even though I could now, I don't go out in public and

I haven't gone back to the river. I avoid familiar places. But being out, having a phone in the house that rings sometimes, even if it is just someone trying to sell something, and being out on the road at night, which I do to keep from going totally loony, brings it home that Kristen is really gone. All the time I was in there, without even thinking about it, I assumed that if I got out, the world would get back to normal.

But it hasn't.

Natalie

That little weasel is out of jail. Can you believe it? They just let him out to walk around free and plot another perverted murder. At least now everyone knows about him and it's not so likely that anyone will be suckered into being alone with him the way Kristen was. We found out his dad's address. One of Kristen's Honor Society friends who's a TA looked it up in the school records. I heard some kids at school talking about egging the house this weekend. I'd go with them in a minute, but Brad is taking me to Seattle.

School is almost over and I'll be a senior. Less than two weeks to go. It's really hectic, especially Smith's class. He assigns all this stuff, like English is the only class we have. I also got a good summer job in the port office. I'll answer the phone and collect moorage money from people for their yachts. It pays ten dollars an hour, so I could make enough over the summer to buy a cheap car. Trish says she thinks she can afford insurance on the Granada now, so I can be added to the policy. I'm pretty excited about it. It's part of why I made the decision I did.

I haven't told him, so it will be a big surprise for Brad. I hope he likes it. It's a huge change for me and I'm pretty nervous about it, but I have an appointment after school today to get my hair cut and dyed back to my natural color. I can't believe I'm doing it. Weird hair has been my trademark since middle school. It's what people expect from me. Maybe it's part of what Brad likes about me and he'll be mad that I changed it, but it was part of the deal for the job. Our relationship shouldn't be about hair anyway.

I was lucky to get the interview. A lot of people applied, but I got some teachers to write letters. Smith wrote a really good one. I heard that he doesn't think Corey did it. I don't blame him too much and I still like him. Teachers are kind of like ministers. It's their job to be nice, even to slime balls.

It was pretty easy to talk to them at the port and I know I can do a good job. So I'm sitting there in the office answering their questions, the port manager and the lady who runs the office, and it feels pretty good. They seem to like me okay, and I can tell it's winding down, when the guy looks me in the eye and says, "How important is your hair?"

And I had to decide in that instant, because I could tell from the way he asked that I probably wouldn't get the job with maroon hair. So I said, "I'm planning to change it back to its original color. It's kind of brown. This color is just a phase I've been going through, to be different. I guess I've outgrown it."

So they gave me the job and I have to go through with the big change. It took a while, but I found a picture of myself with my natural hair color to take to the beauty shop. It's funny. While I was looking, I found all these pictures of Kristen and me in the drawer. We look so different. I mean she's all girly and preppy and I'm all punk and rebellious-looking. She's been gone for two months and I just keep missing her more. The thing I heard is that when people die, sometimes the people closest to them start acting like them. Like their brothers or sisters take on some of their personality traits to fill in the empty spot they left. Maybe that's why I'm changing my hair. I bought some new clothes the other day too, including something to wear to the wedding. It was like she was with me, helping me choose, and what I bought is a lot more normal-looking than what I usually wear.

Brad may not recognize me on Saturday.

Kristen

The blinds were open because I like the light. My bedroom window faces the street and I was expecting him. Whenever I heard a car, I looked to see if it was him. I'd been seeing a lot of him. When we were with other people, he made jokes about me being his long-lost niece. Grant told me I made him happy. I filled a gap in his life that he hadn't even known was there. It was great. It was like the poverty part was gone from my pretend vacation.

He took me back to the museum. It felt like being there with an uncle or a teacher. He knows a lot about Native American and natural history. Most of the time, that's the way it was, like being on a family outing but without all the tension I would feel when I was with Bonnie and Sterling. He treated me like I was his favorite daughter. I got his full attention. We also went to the Butchart Gardens like he promised, even though the roses weren't blooming yet. I love that sunken part that was once a rock quarry.

Time with him passed quickly and I grew more comfortable with him, and it was easy to say yes when he suggested doing something. I wouldn't have given it much thought except for what happened after the bike ride with Leigh.

My spending an afternoon with Leigh wasn't even a real date. I hadn't talked to him for quite a while, but one day when we were having a slow afternoon, he asked how my bike was working now, and if I ever rode on trails. I hadn't, of course. I didn't think I wanted anything to do with trails from what I'd seen of those guys in their football armor at Whistler and the stories I heard from some of the guys at school who ride like that.

"The place I'm thinking about is different," Leigh said. "The trail we would go on is really flat and wide, more like a logging road."

So I went with him. He let me use an old mountain bike that he kept for riding on the street. It didn't have shock absorbers, but the tires were wide and worked better on gravel than the skinny tires on my bike would have. It was nice to get off of city streets. Even though he is quite a bit older than me and is mature enough to be running the restaurant, he has this young attitude. He likes mountain biking and rock climbing and travels around the world with his buddies to do those things. He said he doesn't want to worry about a career yet or about having to settle down, because he doesn't know what the career would be, and he's having a lot of fun. He tried college, but he just couldn't get into it, so now he's working for his dad, saving up money for another trip.

We had fun riding and talking. It was all very innocent. It would have just been another good day in my great adventure and part of what made it harder and harder to think about going back, except for what happened when he dropped me off. I noticed the white SUV right away when we turned onto my street. It was parked across from the house. We had stopped to eat on the way back and Leigh was meeting friends at a pub, so he just dropped me off and kept going. Grant stayed in the car until he was gone.

"Where have you been?"

His voice had an edge that made me think of Sterling. The first thought that came to mind was that I shouldn't have to tell him. So I answered, "On a date."

"So, who's the lucky guy? Do I get to meet him?"

"It was no big deal. We went on a bike ride. I know him from work. He's my boss."

"He looks young to be your boss."

"He's still kind of a kid, like me, but he's a good boss. We had a good time."

"When you weren't here, I got worried. I even stopped by the restaurant."

Then he changed the subject. It was instant and complete.

"I've got tickets to a show tomorrow night. It's a rare opportunity for us. A dance troupe from New York at the Royal Theater. I really want you to see this. It's quite special. We can go to dinner first." He seemed pretty excited about it.

I agreed to go with him, but then I began to have doubts. I had nothing to wear and he offered to take me shopping, but I decided to decline his offer. It's funny how some little thing, a detail, can change the way you see something. The exchange of a few words and a particular tone of voice and my view of Grant had changed. He had been good to me and I didn't want to hurt him, but in spite of his insistence that we were just friends, it was clear now that he was courting me, even though he hadn't tried to kiss me romantically or tried anything else. He was jealous of Leigh.

In spite of all the favorite-niece-and-friend talk, he treated me like we were dating. He opened doors for me and held my chair in restaurants. He touched my back, my arm, my hands, but he never put his hand on my thigh or anywhere private. He had kissed me on the forehead. It had made me uncomfortable because he stayed close, inhaled deeply and said he loved the way I smelled. But he has this way of gracefully backing off and putting you at ease when you start to feel threatened. I should have seen it sooner, but I let myself get seduced even if it wasn't about sex yet. After meeting him, I continued going to work, of course, but didn't see much of my roommates. Biking with Leigh was really the first break, the first chance to break the spell, and now it's broken.

Everyone I know here thinks he's a relative, and that I'm making the connections I told them I came here for. But he's not family. He's twice my age. I hadn't asked him if he was married, at least not point blank the way Natalie would have. My courage for that kind of thing comes and goes, and bringing up that topic would have cut through the favorite-niece game. If Natalie had found a birth certificate that raised all those questions about who she was, she would have homed in on the person who could answer them and created a storm that wouldn't quit until everything was out in the open.

Grant is evasive. Bonnie is too, but in a different way. Grant can talk for hours and keep you interested without revealing anything about himself. I recognize this kind of deceit because here, I can't reveal anything about myself either. The woman's clothes I saw in his car that first day when we put the bike in the back made me think he must be married. I asked him about the dress and blouse to give him a chance to tell me about his family, and he said the clothes belonged to a friend, a neighbor. If he has a wife, she's either out of town, or she gives him lots of space. So does his job. He has a lot of free time. Besides knowing Victoria, he knows Vancouver too. Maybe he really lives there and comes here on business. Maybe he's a lobbyist or has something to do with the government and has this family back in Vancouver. I learned more about Leigh's life in one afternoon than I have about Grant in several weeks.

So that night, the night we had our moment of truth, I was in my room waiting. I heard a car and saw the Cadillac pull up. It's a quiet street with big shade trees evenly spaced. I watched Grant come up to the front door. He was carrying flowers, yellow roses. I knew it wasn't going to be easy.

On the way to the restaurant, he did most of the talking, telling me about the dance troupe and why the chance to see them was so special. I ordered my usual pear cider and drank it down like I was thirsty, then got most of the way through another before I was able to say it.

"Grant, these past weeks have been really great. You're a good friend and you've spent a lot of time with me—"

"This sounds like a prelude to something sad. Let's not be sad."

The cider was pretty strong, and I hadn't eaten. The alcohol was finding Natalie's bluntness for me.

"It doesn't have to be sad, Grant. I just need some space. I've been spending nearly all my free time with you. I miss having time alone. I miss people my own age."

"Of course you're right, Amy. What's happened between us is highly unusual and happened very quickly. You should have time for your friends, but you've become such an important part of my life, it will be hard for me. Yesterday when you went off with that young man, it was torture."

"That's what I mean. It shouldn't be torture. I'm not your wife or your girlfriend, and I don't want to be. I'm not your niece. I don't really know anything about you except that you've been nice to me. For all I know, you have a wife and family somewhere that you should be spending your time with. I've enjoyed your company, but I had fun yesterday with Leigh and I shouldn't need your approval if I want to go out with someone my own age."

"I see. You've fallen for him and you're dumping me. That's what you'd call it isn't it? Dumping?"

Even cushioned by the cider, it was clear that he had changed. His eyes were hard. No sign of the usual smooth slide onto a more pleasant topic. The waitress came for our order. He snapped at her, icy voiced, to give us more time. He was like Sterling.

"Grant, I can't dump you. We're not going together. We're not in love. I need a friend. Friends give each other time and space. Friends tell each other about their lives. I'm going through some hard stuff right now. You've been nice to me. You said you were my friend and I believed you. I wanted it to be true. I wanted to believe that someone could be nice to me just because he liked me."

While I was talking, I flashed back to the feeling I had the first night at the restaurant in Brentwood Bay. The feeling about how that particular moment was the result of so many unlikely moments that it deserved the truth, or at least I had to be willing to tell the truth if I was asking for honesty from him. It had to be fair. If he had told me honestly about his life, then I would have had to tell him about mine. I had to be willing to go back to the Valley and to life with Bonnie and Sterling, if that's where the truth took me. I had to be willing to know the truth about the birth certificate, about my real father, however unpleasant it ended up being.

I said, "I just want the truth. I don't care if you're married. I don't care if you are trying to seduce me, which is what I think right now. Just tell me the truth. No more pretense about me being your long-lost favorite niece."

"You're such an innocent," is what he said. His eyes were still cold. They drilled into me and I shivered.

"Are you married?"

He laughed. He sounded bitter.

"Tell me about your job. What's it like? Do you work for the government?"

The waitress came back.

"Order something," he said softly, but I could feel the hardness behind the words, and it scared me. I ordered a chicken dish.

He ordered lamb.

Then he changed back and started talking about New York and how, the last time he was there, he saw the dance troupe that was performing tonight.

"It was a spectacular performance and even if they aren't as good tonight as they were in New York—traveling companies can be inconsistent—it will still be a good show." His eyes warmed and he told me I would like the chicken dish, that it was quite good. It made me think of Bonnie and my few attempts to get her to talk about my real father.

"Grant, did your wife die?"

His eyes drilled and I shivered again and got quiet. I ate a piece of bread. When the chicken finally came, I tried to eat. He was right, it was good, but I couldn't eat it. His plate had this circular rack of bones sticking up and I couldn't help but think of lambs and butchering and honesty and how much of life is based on pretense.

"We're not friends," I said. "And I don't think you ever wanted to be."

"You're such a fool," he said, "a beautiful little fool."

"That may be true," I said, "but I'm not staying here any longer, and I'm not going to your goddamned ballet." I said it quietly so as not to make a scene. I picked up my purse from the floor next to my chair and stood to leave. To anyone watching, I could have been going to the bathroom. He didn't look up, but paused and said,

"Pity."

It made me feel crawly all over. Then he looked up at me and said, "Such a shame."

The way he said it scared the crap out of me, but I kept my cool and walked out.

It would have been a long walk back to the house. I had enough money with me for a taxi but had never been in one before; they're not that common in the Valley. From the movies, and I felt like I was in a movie, it didn't seem like hailing one would be that hard. I didn't know what to expect from Grant, but I had a very bad feeling and was glad there were a lot of people around as I walked down to the harbor in front of the Empress and got a cab.

I was relieved to find Ian and Char home. They were eating

Easy Mac and drinking Molson's.

"Thought you were out with that rich relative," Ian said.

"He's not really my relative. I thought he was, but I found out he really isn't."

"Too bad. So will you be giving up the high life to watch the tube with us tonight?"

"Do you mind?"

I don't sleep much now, and even though the room is dark and the blinds are thick enough that you can barely see silhouettes through them and are always pulled, I have this feeling of being watched. Often, after a couple hours of tossing around, I get up and peek outside. Sometimes I'm sure I see Grant's SUV parked in the shadows down the street.

Natalie

Trish stuck around to watch Brad's reaction to the new me. She was going off to do something with one of her friends, but drank another cup of coffee and fussed around the kitchen until he came. She can be like a kid sometimes, and even with her skepticism about Brad and me, this was too good to miss. It was pretty fun. I mean when I answered the door, he was shocked. He just stood there like he didn't recognize me but sort of did, so he didn't know whether or not to ask this stranger if I was home. He was truly speechless, which was cool because you hear that expression all the time when it's not quite true, but he really couldn't speak until Trish started laughing and said, "It's her."

Trish has a good heart and can't stand to see anyone uncomfortable for very long. What Brad said was, "Wow!"

Which I will never forget and thought was absolutely cool because I could tell he wasn't just being polite. He likes the new me. So I was really happy and looking forward to his cousin's wedding where maybe he would be proud to be with me, and to the evening when it would be more relaxed.

The wedding was on this small ship called the Virginia V. It's really old and powered by steam, so even though the engine is right out in the open where you can see it in this kind of pit in the middle of the main deck, it's really quiet. You can stand beside it and talk. The engine is also spotless; you could eat off of it, and the rest of the boat is like brand new too, even though it's nearly a hundred years old. It was a passenger and freight boat on Puget Sound back in the day.

Once the groom had kissed the bride and the ceremony was over, the boat went through the ship canal into Lake Washington. The reception started with people telling stories, some of them funny, about the bride or the groom, or about them as a couple. As we cruised the shoreline, people got into a food line on the main deck or danced on the upper deck. It was a good party, and I thought it was a nice way to have a wedding. Since I had already seen some of the houses along the shore from Brad's boat, I knew what to expect, but it was still fun to look and to imagine what it would be like to live in some of those places.

Brad and I were sitting at a table by the window. The boat was getting close to his house when he said he needed to go to the bathroom, then was going to go back and get some more food. I had eaten enough and was happy looking out the window. It was a perfect day, not too hot or cold or windy, and there were boats on the water pulling skiers or inner tubes, people having fun, families having a day together with kids who waved as we passed. I was having fun too.

Then Jean, Brad's mother, came and sat down next to me.

"Hello, deary, I see you've changed your look."

I don't know if it's because my first knowledge of her is connected to the fear I felt when I didn't know Brad and thought he was going to rape me, or because she's just plain cold to me, but she makes me feel off balance, like when guys set off my creep alarm. She's beautiful, but she oozes bad vibes, danger.

My first vision of her was in my imagination that night in the car when Brad was persuading me he wasn't a killer pervert by explaining what had happened that day. I pictured her naked, like in a sex scene from a movie. Her face was featureless and this wrestling coach, jock guy was grunting away on top of her as Brad walked in. I'm used to being pretty blunt, but because of Brad, I have to be careful when I talk to her. She's still his mom and he has to work through his disappointment without me complicating it for him. Being tactful without lying is new to me, so it takes my full concentration and I don't have a lot of confidence.

"Yeah. I guess it was time."

"Did you change for Brad?"

"It was to get a job so I can buy a car."

"Oh yes. That cute little town you live in probably doesn't have public transportation. We went to see the tulips once when Brad was little. But you live with the Indians, don't you? Are you part Indian?"

"Not that I know of. My aunt's husband is Native."

"You and Brad are spending a lot of time together."

"That's true." I wanted to say that he was becoming my best friend and that he was one of the nicest people I'd ever known, but I checked myself.

"Well, Natalie, Brad seems quite smitten with you. A mother can tell. So there's something I want you to know now, before this goes any further. Don't for a minute get any ideas about marrying him or slithering in and becoming part of all this. Bradley's last name may be Stanfield, but he's also a Whitfield. And I didn't raise my son to waste his life with some little tramp who thinks she can get her hooks into his money through his innocent heart or by having his baby.

"I'm putting the burden on you. If he tries to marry you, or if you get pregnant with his baby, I will disinherit him, kick him out of the family, and you will be responsible. So have your little fling, but know that it's temporary, and be very careful."

I couldn't help it. I knew better. I was careful how I worded it, and was kind of proud about how it came out.

"So I get to be Brad's version of your wrestling coach friend as long as it's temporary and not messy, but if we happen to connect and it lasts and maybe we find trust and friendship or even love... I don't want your money. I don't want your life. It sounds like you're trying to raise Brad to be as miserable as you are, but you're failing. He's screwing up and might actually turn out happy. You're stepping in to try and ruin it. I don't think you can ruin it by taking away money. I think Brad's bigger than that. But we're really just kids. We're trying to be friends, having a little cross-cultural experience. You don't need to panic yet."

Our exchange was happening quietly. The music and laughter covered our voices enough so that when Brad came up with his plate of food, we could have been talking about the weather. Except for the look on his mother's face. She was pissed. She was facing away from him, and I don't think he noticed. Her practiced smile returned instantly when she saw my eyes shift to him, and she rose from the chair, putting her hand on his shoulder as they exchanged places.

"What was that about?" he asked.

"She's just being a mom, worrying about her boy, not wanting him to be taken advantage of by scheming girls. I don't think she likes me."

"What did she say?"

"Nothing, Brad. Let it go. She was just making sure that my intentions are honorable."

"What would she know about honor."

The good part is that we were able to drop it. The rest of his relatives were nice to me. We even danced a little and had a good time. We were pretty tired when the boat docked, but decided to go to the ball game anyway because the stadium was a neutral place and not very crowded since the Mariners were on a losing streak. The captain of the Virginia V let us change out of our wedding clothes in the stateroom behind the pilothouse while the caterers were clearing their stuff off the boat, so we were dressed comfortably for the game.

The Mariners surprised us by winning and I called Trish to let her know I was spending the night on Brad's couch, which I did, but when I kissed him goodnight before he went into his room, it lasted a long time and it was hard to sleep, lying there in that big house and thinking about him so close on the other side of the door, but knowing his mom was upstairs, hating me. He took me home in the morning and I didn't see his mother.

Kristen

After I walked out on him in the restaurant, the first time I saw Grant's car parked on our street late at night, I picked up the phone and came very close to dialing. I would have called Natalie, not Bonnie, even though I knew I would end up calling Bonnie too after Natalie helped me build up my courage. I was totally unnerved. But I didn't call. I'm trying to be cool about it, but I'm scared. I mean who wouldn't be. Grant's stalking me. I began thinking about going back; I actually wanted to.

But I'm trying to think it through, problem-solve the way they teach us at school. I have a lot at stake. Going back would be huge. These months of being on my own have made me think a lot. If I'm not ready, stepping back into the Valley will be like falling into the abyss—"the valley and the shadow," from the Bible. I have to go back strong enough to "fear no evil," which means standing up to Bonnie and making her tell me the truth about my real dad, and telling her what I really think about Sterling and church and politics, and what I feel about life.

Strange as it may sound, I'm just as afraid of going back to my old life and pretending to be someone I'm not as I am of anything Grant could do to me. At least, in his twisted way, Grant is being honest now.

If I can't go back to Bonnie and Sterling strong enough to come out of the closet, so to speak, it will be worse than if I had just stayed in there, because I've broken all the rules. It took strength to confront Grant about being straight with me, and I got what I asked for, a more honest relationship. Now I know where I really stand, and even though he totally creeps me out, I know who he really is. I got myself into this, by being stupid and by being brave, and I'm trying to handle it like an adult and find the best way out.

Sometimes when I'm lying in bed and I have the feeling that he's out there, my mind bounces around inside my skull like a trapped bee. My imagination runs wild with possibilities. There are plenty of true stories, and a lot of them happened near enough to cut through any sense of safety-by-distance I might try to create. Besides Ted Bundy and that Green River guy, who had a wife and a regular job and still killed dozens of girls, there's that pig farmer guy in Vancouver who killed women and fed the bodies to his pigs, and those sniper guys who killed people in Seattle because of the older guy's bad marriage. So I lie in bed trying to guess what Grant is thinking. Every sound and every shadow that moves make my heart pound.

Sometimes I'm so scared I cry, and sometimes I get really angry and plot ways to reverse the situation. I've been told all my life that when I'm in danger, I'm supposed to "get help," like there was a Batman or a Zorro out there for all of life's problems. When I started cutting myself, I knew it wasn't normal and I tried to think of an adult who could show me where to "get help." I thought a lot about whom I could tell, but there really wasn't anyone.

You'd think a school counselor might be a good option, since they're supposed to be trained to handle emotional stuff. Mrs. Tollefson is nice enough, and great when it comes to helping you think about a career or what college to go to, but if I had told her, it would immediately have gotten back to Bonnie and Sterling. Mrs. Tollefson would have assigned me to some shrink, which might not have been bad if it was the right person, but since Bonnie and Sterling would know, it would have gotten even more stressful. It would be like being in a war and telling your secrets to your enemy so they could use them against you, like me asking Grant to help me figure out how to protect myself against him.

I thought about telling Mr. Smith by writing about it in my journal. He at least didn't feel like the enemy, but he told us at the beginning of the year that he's required by law to report anything we write about being abused or about things that might endanger us, including suicide, and he could get fired if he doesn't, so that would have been just like going to Mrs. Tollefson.

I've run my options through my mind. If I was still in the Valley with nothing to lose, calling the police would be my first thought. What if I call the police? It will mean answering a lot of questions and filling out forms. As soon as I pick up the phone, I might as well be calling Bonnie too. So I have to consider that and be prepared for it, but that's not the biggest problem. Grant hasn't done anything illegal. He hasn't threatened me. He hasn't tried to break into my house. He just makes himself visible at times and in ways that scare me.

He doesn't park on our street every night and when he does, he doesn't stay all night, but he does it at times that I'm likely to see the car. It gives me the willies. I get this feeling that I'm being watched sometimes while I'm riding my bike to or from work, and I've quit going to the park altogether. I hang out with Ian and Char and their friends as much as I can, which I'm sure they think is a little strange, but they've been good about it. I try to stay in public places when I'm alone. I know he follows me. I see his car way too often. Sometimes it's parked near the restaurant.

Now he's started actually coming in, getting a table and ordering food when I'm on shift. He doesn't stare at me or do anything obviously creepy. He doesn't pretend he doesn't know me either, which would scare me more. In fact, he's polite, but his eyes are cold. He calls me by name and treats me the way someone would if he was a regular customer. He tips exactly eighteen percent.

So, if I call the cops, what would I tell them? When my imagination runs wild I get really scared, and I've had the phone in my hand more than once. I imagine the conversation going either of two ways. I could get a nice lady cop who would be all sympathetic. I could just tell her the story, and she would let me know that I had been a little stupid, but she would be understanding, even though I couldn't tell her that I wouldn't have gotten into the car with him that first day except for all the good luck I was having with people. The nice lady cop I imagine wouldn't want to know my life history or see my ID, but she still would end up saying that since Grant hadn't done anything yet, there wasn't much the police could do. She would start a file and maybe send a patrol car down my street once in a while.

The other extreme would be some pushy guy like Sterling who would want my life story and would make me feel like an idiot, which I don't need because I feel that way already.

So it's kind of strange. If Grant doesn't kill me and throw my body in the Strait or turn it into pellets and feed it to the geese in the park or something like that, there is a good side to all this. There was that moment in the restaurant, the moment of truth, so to speak. I was brave and didn't back down, and even though I had help from the cider, I did what Natalie does all the time: I said what I thought. I was really scared, but I went through with it anyway, and I'm proud of myself even if it did make my life worse.

Corey

I know he smells it. I have the door open and he's on the porch. The music is still too loud and the song is about being comfortably numb. Before he knocked, I was trying to get that way. Good thing I was just getting started. Luckily, I'm okay to talk, not like sometimes.

"You know this one, Mr. Smith. I've heard you listening to it too, after school, so it's like I'm doing homework. I was pretty amazed when you played the part about them trashing the school in class."

"That's part of why I'm here, Corey. It looks like you're passing all of your classes. You've been doing your homework and have surprised some of the teachers. Congratulations."

I invite him in and get him to sit down in my dad's chair, then turn down the music. I notice he's wearing blue jeans and hiking shoes instead of the usual khakis and polo.

"It's kind of weird, huh. But besides you, the only other person who's been nice to me is the school lady at Juvie. She said I could get enough credits to graduate by the end of next year. It's not like I really believe it matters, graduation, I mean, but the school work passes the time, like getting high, only it doesn't make me as hungry. Pretty ironic, huh?"

"Corey, remember what I said about being a short-timer and how it makes me want to cut through the bull?"

"You were right about there being different ways to be trapped. I'm going crazy here, Mr. Smith. I've got nothing to do. I do homework because sometimes it takes my mind off things, and I guess it's good to hear that they noticed and it messes with their heads a little. But sometimes I need to get high. I don't smoke much."

He's looking at me like he's not so sure.

"I saw that it was you out the window and knew you could hear the music. I knew you'd smell it too, so I wasn't going to answer the door. Yeah, I remember what you said about the bull. That's why I let you in. You were straight with me. Try to understand. Remember what you said you felt sometimes about wishing the uncertainty was over? Sometimes I think I'm going to blow, like I know what those guys in the Middle East are feeling when they strap on the bombs. I just want to end it. I'm not there yet, like I'm not ready to kill myself today or anything, but sometimes I get close. In the hospital they put you out so you don't feel so much pain. I don't see how this is all that different."

I'm on the couch, across the room from him. The light from the window is reflecting off his glasses so I can't tell from his eyes what he's thinking. He's smaller than my dad and doesn't have a potbelly. When my dad and I watch TV together, although we rarely do, this is where we sit, so sitting here with Mr. Smith feels a little odd.

"I'm not here to judge you, Corey. You're in a tough spot, and you have to find your own way through it. But I worry about you. You're in enough trouble without this, and will probably need a clear head to see a way out. You might get too comfortable in the ozone. Even with doctors around, medication can be dangerous. When pain doesn't make you give up, it can make you fight harder."

I guess it's lecture time, but since it's Smith and he's the closest thing to a friend I've got now, I'm being polite.

"Look," he says, "I'll tell you something the doctor told me, back in the beginning when I asked him what my odds were. He told me to live like I was going to win, then make adjustments only when it became absolutely necessary. What I took it to mean was that I shouldn't give up and act like I was beaten until I truly was. That as long as I could walk, talk, eat and breathe, it was a good day. But mainly, even on bad days, as long as there was hope that I could get some good days again, I should fight for them."

"You've got something to fight for, Mr. Smith. Everyone likes you. The whole world thinks I'm a pervert. Even my sister. If Kristen showed up alive tomorrow, I still couldn't go back to that fucking school. I didn't do it, and I hate those bastards for believing I did. I'm trying, Mr. Smith, but there isn't much to hope for. Smoking a little and listening to music is as close to a good day as it gets for me. I want out of this stinking place so fucking bad."

"Where would you go if you could leave?"

"I dream about camping on the beach in Mexico, but I don't have any money and I don't speak Spanish."

"Is there anyone, a relative, you could go stay with where you could get a fresh start?"

"Come on. Would you let a pervert stay at your house?"

"What if you were cleared?"

"Fat chance. Besides, I'm not that close to anyone. They all thought I was trouble before."

"Well, they don't have enough evidence to charge you. Once you turn eighteen and you deal with the drug charge, they can't make you stay around here. When will you be eighteen?"

"Not until next February."

"If you knew you could leave in February, do you think you could last?"

"I don't know. It would be hard. I feel like I'm going to pop."

"Mexico's a good thought, but like you said, it would take money and Spanish. Let's come up with a plan that could work. If you had three thousand dollars to get started on a new life, where would you go?"

"Where am I going to get that kind of money?"

"You've been dreaming about Mexico. Just shift the dream a little. Work out real details. Figure out bus fare or plane fare, or if you hitched, food and a place to stay. You feel like you're going to pop. That's real, and fair enough. You're in a trap. So, plan an escape. Like a prison break. Remember Huck Finn. He was trapped and he ran. It's a big world out there. If you stay and go over the edge, you lose. If you attempt to build a new life and fail, at least you tried. One of my high school friends left home after graduation with a tooth brush and seventy-eight cents. He's teaching at a community college in California now. I have another high school friend who took off like that and drank himself to death in Florida. So you can lose too, but sometimes people win. So, where would you go if you had some money?"

"I'd have to rob a bank. I have seventy-eight cents and a tooth brush, and I've thought about it a lot, and I might disappear if I don't come unglued first. But to me the result seems about the same. I'm a loser either way."

"I'm going to make you an offer."

"Why do you care what happens to me?

"Maybe you remind me a little of myself. My offer is a loan, and there are strings, but nothing that should compromise your integrity. Listen for a minute. I just sold a boat. It wasn't worth a lot, but it might be enough. I was going to use the money as a down payment on a better pickup, but I'm willing to gamble on you. I'm offering to loan you the three thousand dollars I got for my boat so you can get away from here and make a new start in life. I expect you to pay it back someday when you have a job and can afford payments. You don't have to sign a paper, and if you don't pay it back, I won't send a collection agency."

"You'd loan me money? I don't get it."

"If you really think you're about to go off the deep end, take the money and go away somewhere. Start over. You're young. You can. Seeing you get through this is more important to me now than driving a new truck. I can live with my old one. It still works fine. You decide if and when you need the money, and if and when you can pay it back. It's a way out. But you can't just draw on it for spending money."

"Why are you doing this? People don't care about other people without a reason. You're not gay or anything, are you? I mean if you're here because you want me to give you a blowjob, I won't do it."

"No, Corey. That's not it."

"So why? I guess I can believe you think I didn't kill her, because I didn't, and someone should believe the truth. But people don't go around offering money. I mean that's just stupid. You don't seem stupid."

"It would be a deal between two people on the edge, trying to hang on. A matter of trust. You're right. When something is true, someone, someplace, should believe it. That's why I'm offering. Maybe I am stupid. I believe you have integrity. If you take the money, it becomes a responsibility, a connection. You're stuck with what it represents—someone believes in you enough to take a three-thousand-dollar chance. It will become part of your baggage like it became part of mine."

"What do you mean?"

"Someone believed in me once when I thought no one did. I had burned some bridges and had some bad luck. Part of it was about a girl and part of it was about my parents. I felt like I didn't have much to live for and I was pretty mad at the world. I was a little older than you, but the person who believed in me was a teacher. It changed my life. So maybe my offer is a way to repay a debt."

"You'd actually hand me three thousand dollars cash?"

"I'd probably give you a check, just to make you go to the

bank. It depends on the circumstances. If you truly needed cash, I would get you cash. To do it right, you should open an account, maybe get a debit card, keep track of the money, use it carefully."

"What if I used it to buy drugs or a gun, or stuff to make a bomb?"

"Then I might be in trouble. At best I'd feel really stupid. I know I'm taking a chance. This is about trust. Trust is one of those important abstract things I talk about in class. For it to be real, someone needs to believe in it enough to risk it, put their money where their mouth is. I'm willing to bet three thousand dollars on you. In the big picture, it's not very much. It could backfire. If you take it and don't use it in good faith, it will make you feel guilty, give you one more reason to get stoned, to feel like a loser, to quit. If you're not willing to bet on yourself, you shouldn't take it."

He gets up. I can tell it's hard for him to get out of the chair, like his back hurts or something. He moves toward the door.

"You don't need to decide now," he says. "You may not need it. But it's there. It's part of your reality now, your baggage, one of the things you'll carry with you. I hope it helps. I can listen too. So if you find yourself ready to let go, even if you don't want the money, call me."

And he left. Just like that. And I'm sitting there, not quite sure what just happened, even more confused than the last time I saw him. I turn the music back up loud, but don't smoke any more that day.

Kristen

Courage is a funny thing. It took a lot of courage for me to stand up to Grant. But I think bravery is really desperation, and when you choose the thing that may appear bold to other people, you know inside that there's really more danger in the other choices. Even though I couldn't have said it at the time, I had to escape Bonnie and Sterling because I couldn't stand trading my honesty for comfort. I couldn't face my life the way it was. I ended up in the same situation with Grant, like I was drawn there because it was familiar, and I knew how to act because I had been there before. It was easier to believe his talk and pretend it was true than to face the real truth. There were rewards for pretending. But when I let myself see him for what he is, I didn't feel very good about myself.

I guess I learned I'm sick of pretending. I think it costs too much and I don't want to do it any more. I got the truth from Grant. He's a creep, and even though I'm trying to handle it like an adult, I'm really scared. If Grant doesn't get me first, I have to go back. Both things scare me. The idea of going back feels right and it also terrifies me. But I know it's the only way I can have the kind of life I want.

When I imagine it, dialing the phone or just showing up, my heart starts beating fast and I get just as scared as I do when I lie awake at night imagining Grant lurking outside my window. I play out the possibilities in my head: if it was just Bonnie, I could have done it already, easily. The scariest thing about Bonnie is that you can't touch her. For me, the valve of her attention seems shut tight. But I also know there is a bond between us, even if I don't understand completely how it got there.

Bonnie isn't just Bonnie. I can't remember when she was just Bonnie. She's Bonnie and Sterling. She's connected herself to him and she hides behind him. When I imagine returning to her, imagine the moment when the door opens for me at their house, it's always Sterling who opens it, and it's his anger I face while Bonnie remains in the shadows.

So I've been putting it off. With Grant, I know what I'm scared of, although it seemed to be changing. He hasn't been to the restaurant for several days and I hadn't seen his car, so I'd been hoping that he'd lost interest in me and I could take my time planning my return. Except for the business with Grant, I've liked Victoria, and it will be hard to leave.

At about four this afternoon, the restaurant was nearly empty, so I took advantage of the lull and rode home on the bike to get some different clothes. I planned to go straight from the restaurant to meet Ian and Char at a pub. I rounded the corner onto our street and there it was. That white SUV was parked directly across the street from the house.

I stopped the bike to see if Grant was in it, but I couldn't tell. Other parked cars blocked my view. I waited, heart racing, wondering if he'd already seen me. Then I made up my mind. I assumed he was in the car and that he had seen me, so I decided I would ride past him and look him in the eye, but I wouldn't stop. Maybe it was a crazy idea, but I had learned from cutting myself that what you imagine is sometimes worse than the actual experience, so I wanted to look in his eyes and get that sharp, clean rush of adrenaline that I get when the blade breaks the skin. Since his car was facing me, he couldn't pull out and turn around before I got to the corner. If he got out and chased me on foot, I could outrun him on the bike.

The car was empty. I could see that before I got to it, so I looked for him in our yard. If he was snooping around, he was in the back or, worse, inside. There was no dust on the Escalade. He must take it through the car wash every day. As I rode past, I looked in and saw a pair of binoculars on the passenger seat, and wondered if they had night vision.

I rode as fast as I could back to the restaurant. Business was still slow and Leigh saw me come in. I was sweating and out of breath, so I went into the restroom to straighten up. When I came out, he was waiting.

"Are you all right?"

"I'm not sure," I said. He took me back to his office, which was even more cluttered than it was when he interviewed me. I sat across from him in the same chair.

"Well?"

"I'm okay," I said. "I just had a little scare."

I was about to make up a lie about a near miss in traffic, but then I made the decision. I decided to disappear again. I didn't tell him the whole truth, but I told him enough that he offered to go back to the house with me after work so I could get some things, and to let me sleep on his couch tonight. He wanted to confront Grant. He has some friends that he said would enjoy letting Grant know what it feels like to be stalked. I told him to wait a few days, and if Grant didn't stay away, I would call the police.

It's really late now but I can't sleep, though I know I should. Leigh gave me a pillow and some blankets and his couch is comfortable and clean. My mind is swirling. I keep imagining being face to face with Sterling and Bonnie. I run through various plans in my head. There's only one ferry to Anacortes each day and it leaves Sidney at 11:20 a.m. Going back the way I came would be the simplest thing to do. I've got a bus schedule and it would be easy to just get up in the morning and go to the bus stop. I'm supposed to start work at ten tomorrow morning, and since Leigh closed up last night, he's going in late too, so that complicates that idea. I would have to do more explaining than I want to.

I plan to leave a note saying I went home, so Leigh, Trudy, Ian and Char don't panic and think Grant got me. They all think my home is in Seattle. They've all been nice to me and I'll miss them. I don't want anyone to be able to trace me. Grant thinks my home is in California, which is good. After I've been home for a while, long enough for him to lose interest in me or find someone else to bother, I intend to write and tell the people who were good to me the truth. They deserve that much.

Leigh is being great. I think he's asleep, but you never know. It's quiet in there but I'm being quiet too and I'm wide awake, even with the glass of wine I drank earlier. I'm pretty sure he's courting me too, but he hasn't tried anything yet. Natalie says I'm naïve about boys, now men, and I know she's right, but I also see things in people that she doesn't see, like in Corey. I'm not worried that Leigh will come out here tonight and force me or anything. He has an innocent side too, and part of him really does want to help me, but I can tell he's looking for pay-off.

Once you start fibbing you get trapped, and, because I ran away, I had to tell everyone I met here a fib about myself and who I am. If you only have surface relationships, the fibs don't matter much, but, as soon as you start getting to know someone, it gets complicated. Now I'm getting to know Leigh, and I need his help. So on top of all the other things whizzing around in my head, I'm thinking about him too, and while all this is going on, I feel the need to pee, so I get up.

On my way back to the couch, I go to the window and peek out from between the curtains. It's there! That fucking Escalade! Parked across the street in the shadows, far enough away that you might not notice, but with a direct line of vision to the front windows of the apartment, where I'm standing. I can't see well enough to tell if Grant is in it, but as you might imagine, my heart is pounding in my ears.

I fight the impulse to get Leigh up. Instead, I sit back on the couch with the blankets over me, staring at the curtains. Sometimes you just need someone to share the fright with, but I keep my head and imagine Leigh storming out into the street, which would only lead to trouble and could wind up terrible because either one of them might have a gun. So I stay put and try to think it through. I wish I knew for sure whether Grant is in the car. The apartment has a back door, and I'm imagining slipping out and down the stairs, but he could just as easily be lurking out there somewhere. I put all my stuff in my backpack and tear a sheet of paper from the notebook I write this journal in. I write this note.

Leigh,

In the middle of the night, I made a spur of the moment decision and decided to go home. I left some unfinished business there and this seems like a good time to take care of it. Thanks for the job. Sorry to leave you shorthanded at the restaurant today, but I know you'll find someone to cover. You've been a good friend during a difficult time in my life, so thanks for that too.

Apologize for me to Trudy, Ian and Char for not saying a proper goodbye. They have also been good friends. It's going to be kind of crazy for a while when I get home, so don't expect to hear from me right away, but I will write and explain when things settle down. Don't worry. I'll be fine.

Amy

I put the note under the saltshaker on the table and sit quietly, listening, hoping Leigh is a sound sleeper. It's early morning and the busses will start running soon. I peek through the curtains again and, to my surprise, Grant's car is gone, so I slip out the back door. It squeaks and I shut it carefully and make my way down the stairs and around the building next door, then past the garbage cans to an unlit side street. I left the bike at Ian and Char's, and decide I'm better off without it. I move fast, staying in the shadows, taking a long, indirect route toward a main street where I know there is a bus stop.

Since it's now July, the night is short and light is beginning to show in the eastern sky, over the Valley. East is my direction today. By dark tonight I will have faced the music there.

The city is starting to wake and there are occasional cars. I slide behind trees or bushes when I can, like Corey described. When I get to the bus stop, I stay in the shadow of a building and wait, watching the cars, watching for the Escalade.

I still plan to take the ferry from Sidney to Anacortes, but I'll have to kill a lot of time in Sidney since it's so early. When I see the bus, I step out of the shadows, and it comes to a stop. It's nearly empty. I take a seat toward the back. As it pulls from the curb back into traffic, I recognize by the bike rack the car that pulls alongside. It's Leigh. He sees me and motions for me to come to him, which I understand to mean he wants me to get off at the next stop. I shake my head and look away. He's still following when the bus goes through Sidney, so I don't get off. When it gets to the BC ferry terminal at Schwartz Bay, I have no choice.

According to the schedule, there's a ferry leaving soon. I can get a ticket and get on if I hurry. At the tollbooth, Leigh catches up to me.

"Amy, I got your note. I was worried."

I hug him.

"Sorry I left like that, but I really do need to go back."

"In the middle of the night?"

"Grant's car was out front."

"That asshole! My friends will take care of him. You don't have to go."

"I need to go home and if I don't do it now, I may chicken out. There really is unfinished business."

It's my turn to pay and I buy my ticket. "I've got to go now, Leigh. Really. You've been a good friend when I needed one desperately. I'll write later and explain everything."

"Okay. If I have to, I guess I can accept that. I needed to know directly from you that you're okay, and be sure that it wasn't because of that asshole."

I make it onto the ferry. The Canadian boats have a different look and feel than Washington state ferries. They feel like real ships. When they leave the dock, you get the sense that you're embarking on a voyage, that you're about to cross a vast ocean, heading for another country or somewhere far away, instead of just crossing some lake or canal on a more fun version of a floating bridge. As the foghorn blast announces our departure and the hull shudders beneath me, I decide I am glad Leigh followed me and that I had to change my route home. The world I am heading into will not be the same one I left, and I need time to adjust.

On the boat you can buy a bus ticket to Vancouver. I found the counter, paid and got instructions for boarding. This is the long, complicated route, but it will work and I'm starting early in the day. At the bus station in Vancouver, I'll buy a ticket to Mount Vernon, and take a SKAT bus from there that will drop me off near Natalie's house. I could be home before dark.

Kristen

The distances on the highway signs are in kilometers. When you think about it, borders between countries are pretty strange. Mount Vernon and the Valley are about the same distance from Vancouver as they are from Seattle, but Vancouver is in another country, with different laws and a different way of looking at things. In my mind, as we near the Customs stop, I make rough translations to miles, then estimate minutes left. I'm projecting ahead, imagining what could go wrong. I have a Canadian birth certificate and a fake Washington driver's license. What if they don't let me in?

Am I Canadian or American? Am I Amy Mackenzie or Kristen Nichols? The moment of truth could come at the border. The guy could pull me aside and say, "This license is fake. You're not American. You can't come in." I decided I would make them call Bonnie. This morning I was worried about getting through Customs, but now I'm not. Fate will decide. If they stop me, Bonnie will have to explain it to them and that might be the easiest way for it to play out. If they let me through, I'll have to try to get her to come out from behind Sterling and tell me who I really am. I think that's the part I'm most afraid of.

Well, all my worry about the border crossing was for nothing. I handed the guy my papers and he barely looked at them. After that, the ride down I-5 to Mount Vernon was eerie. It was so familiar; it felt like I had never left. The stretch from the mall at Bellis Fair through Bellingham is where it really hit me. I'd crossed over. I'm back, and it's going to be a long night. I'm wearing sunglasses and a baseball hat, which I wouldn't have worn before. I look different, but someone from school or town might recognize me. I'm glad I sent the note to Natalie. At least it won't be like in Huckleberry Finn where after Huck disappears, Tom thinks Huck is a ghost when he sees him again.

When we arrive in Mount Vernon, I have to wait around for the SKAT bus. I find myself touching the bench to feel the heat of the sun, listening to traffic sounds, scraping my shoe on the pavement to prove to myself that what I'm doing is real. It's late afternoon. It will be dinnertime when I get there, but I'm not hungry. I'm tired from lack of sleep and all the anticipation, but I think that's helping because it makes me kind of numb.

When I left, there were fields of tulips and daffodils. They're gone. Now the picking machines are working the raspberry fields. As the bus crosses the Rainbow Bridge, I look down the channel at the town. It's a pretty town and you can understand why tourists have taken it over. Then I've arrived. The bus stops near the entrance to Shelter Bay, just off the main street that runs through the reservation village.

On the main drag, there are fireworks stands beside the road and kids lighting firecrackers on the sidewalk. The Fourth of July is tomorrow. Independence Day. Natalie's house is on the second street up the hill, parallel to the main street. I will have to walk only a little way, about the distance of a city block. I step off the bus and look straight ahead, hoping no one recognizes me as I walk toward the corner.

On Natalie's street, the old truck is parked in front of his house, between the corner and her house, and he's walking toward it from the front door. It's the old guy who gave me a ride to Anacortes that first morning. He's coming around the tailgate, heading toward the driver's door, and I look down to avoid eye contact, hoping he'll just get in and go away. But he doesn't. He looks right at me with his hand on the door handle and waits until I'm close, then says, "So you decided to come back."

His directness startles me into meeting his eyes. I answer, "It was time."

"I figured you'd come when you was ready." There was warmth in his dark eyes. "They was all pretty worried about you, but I didn't say nothing. I knew you'd be back when you got your job done. They get pretty worked up around here."

Natalie

Okay. This will be hard to describe, but here goes. It was hot and I was glad to be home. It was a busy day at the marina. The job is good and most of the time it's pretty laid back, but not on holidays. It's helping me to understand Brad because people who own yachts have to have at least some money. Like everyone else, some of them are nice and some are complete jerks. Anyway, even though the banks and the post office were open, it was the Fourth of July weekend, although the actual holiday is Tuesday. At work I collected moorage fees from the boats on the transient floats, made my usual Monday run to the bank and picked up the mail at the post office. The town was plugged with tourists, so it was hard to park. Oh yeah, I forgot to say that I got my driver's license because I need it to drive the little pickup on errands for the port.

As usual around the Fourth of July, even though there are only a few stands in the village, the rez sounds like a war zone, with fireworks going off everywhere. Most of the stands are at Boom City out on the highway, and nearly every Native family has some connection to a stand. Everyone has fireworks and none of it is safe and sane. I had skipped lunch and was eating soda crackers with this tuna mix on them (lemon juice, mayo and chopped olives) that Trish had left in the fridge, and was planning to take a shower. Everything felt normal. I mean, I didn't have any unsettled feeling or weird premonition like you might expect just before your reality gets flipped on its head.

There was a knock at the door. This house had a doorbell once, but it hasn't worked for years. I thought it was a neighbor kid or something. I really wasn't thinking much. Trish wasn't home, and I was a little annoyed at the interruption. I wanted to take my shower and call Brad. He had to work that day too, but had the Fourth off. I didn't because it's so busy at the marina, but I would get double time for working the holiday. My mouth was still full of cracker and tuna when I opened the door.

It all happened in an instant. The shock was far worse than the night she left. There was no time to speculate and adjust, to imagine and let it settle. I mean there she was, looking at me. M-80's and rockets exploded in the background, adding noise to our confusion because I don't look like myself and she looked more like me than I do. It took me a moment, and I could easily have choked on the cracker. Instead, I reached up and touched her face with the back of my hand and felt that it was real and warm. I don't remember chewing and swallowing what was in my mouth, but I must have done it because I didn't spit it out, and I was able to say, "You're not dead?"

I really wasn't sure that what I was seeing was real.

"Natalie?"

"Oh Jesus. Kristen. It really is you."

And it was. That's when I learned what people mean when they say they were so surprised they nearly peed their pants. I didn't do it, but now I understand how you can get thrown so off balance, you can lose control. What I did was hug her. And while I was doing it, I cried, really hard, and so did she. We were in the doorway with the door open, crying away. I pulled her into the living room and pushed the door closed.

Finally I blubbered out, "We thought you were dead, but you're really here."

"The letter. Didn't you get the letter?" she said

"What letter?"

"Oh shit. Oh Jesus. Everyone thinks I'm dead? This is really bad."

"They think Corey killed you."

"You were supposed to think I was in Hawaii. I gave this lady a letter to send from there, so that's where they'd look. Oh Jesus, Natalie, I'm sorry. What happened to Corey?"

So I told her everything, about Corey being held in Juvie and how he was out now. Kristen was really upset and wanted to call him right away. I thought she was going to fall apart, like clinically, where we would need to call for real help, but there is definitely something different about her now. She surprised me by pulling herself together so fast. She was strong. I was able to talk her into waiting. As much as I hate Corey, what happened to him is really bad and can't be fixed in an instant with a phone call.

So she settled down, and I was able to tell her about meeting Brad the night she left, and how they searched the drainage ditch beside the lane down by Arlington where he told me about his day. And I told her about me and Brad's mom. Then she told me about changing her look and dressing up like me and getting from the mall to the ferry and working as a waitress, and about meeting that creep and him stalking her and her being brave.

When Brad called, I had to tell him that Kristen was back, but I said her parents didn't even know yet so he couldn't tell a soul, and he was cool about it. Then Trish came home, and when she got over being stunned, we told her a short version of Kristen's story, and she said it was like we were trying to trade lives, which made us laugh. We needed a reason to laugh, because getting Kristen (or Amy. She showed me the birth certificate) through the next part of coming back to life in the Valley was going to be stressful at best.

Trish told her she should think each step through and not do anything that would cause more damage. She knew how much of a shock Kristen's not being dead was to me, and how much adjustment it took even with her sitting in the same room with us where we could actually touch her. We thought it might be better to wait and go see Corey when she could talk to him face to face, or maybe she should just write him. Sometimes emotions can be worked out better on paper. Writing it out can give both people a chance to think more clearly.

I didn't envy Kristen a bit when it came to facing her mom and Sterling. She met it head on. I saw it in her eyes. I watched her find that calm you get when you know you're against the wall and there's nowhere to go. I've been there a few times, and I had to feel some pride for her, going from having all that stuff, the car, the nice house, a free ride to college, to knowing enough about running on empty to keep her head.

"I can't undo it," she said. "So now I have to try and make the best of it. Fix as much as I can. I'll tell Bonnie tonight, and then I'll have to tell the cops. This isn't going to be fun, but all I can do is tell the truth and find a way to make the best of it."

She was right. She was sounding like me, and I didn't envy her situation. I was used to being the strong one. Maybe I was a little hurt, too, to learn that there was a part of her buried so deep inside her that even her best friend, me, didn't know it was there, and that she could do something so huge without trusting me enough to say a word.

When someone you thought was dead comes back to life, at first you're glad they're alive, and then you have to forgive them. But the forgiveness might not last when you find out that all of that pain and grief you suffered, thinking they were dead, was because they simply decided to run away. I believed Kristen about the letter from Hawaii. She believed she had let us know she wasn't dead, and she sent the letter to me and not to her parents, but since it never came, the pain for all of us was as real as it would have been if she had actually been murdered or killed, even if she hadn't intended to make us suffer.

Believing she was dead had really hurt me, and it must

have hurt her mom even more. When I remember the pain of imagining her being raped and murdered, helpless and suffering, and acknowledge how ashamed I feel now for blaming Corey, I won't pretend I'm not angry. But the combination of that pain and the happiness I feel that she is alive will sort itself out. I will forgive her, even though I don't completely understand why she did it. I know she learned something important, and when she came back, she came here first. I know it will eventually make sense.

I told her that I have my license now and I offered her a ride home in Trish's Granada. She thanked me, but asked if she could have a little time alone in my room to collect herself first. I watched a Seinfeld rerun on TV with Trish until she was ready. It's weird how life can seem totally normal, and in an instant everything is different. Then, before you know it, you're back watching TV and it seems like nothing has changed, even though it has.

When she's ready, we go out to the Granada. I drop her off up the street from her house. She thinks it will be easier if they don't know right away that she went to my house first.

Kristen

The letter is probably stuck in the crease of a mailbag in the corner of a post office somewhere. It made me feel awful, learning that everyone believes I'm dead. I think Trudy's friend would have mailed it. It's like that part in Romeo and Juliet when that priest guy is supposed to deliver a letter to Romeo telling him about Juliet faking her death. At least none of us are dead yet.

Natalie looks so different; for a moment I thought I was in the wrong house. I scared her too. Her hand on my cheek... It was one of those moments I'll never forget. By itself, the emotion of seeing her would have been enough, even too much. But what if Corey had killed himself? What if he's thinking about it right now? Everyone thinks he's a murderer and it's my fault, and I need to tell him what happened and how sorry I am. And, I still have to do the one thing I've been dreading most. Maybe it's good that I'm in that zone people talk about, like I'm so numb I'm sort of disconnected from what's happening around me, though not completely.

After I was cried out and took control of my panic and the feeling of helplessness, and accepted that I can't escape what I have to do, I decided that Natalie's right. This is already such a mess, I need to try not to make it worse. I need to do this one step at a time, and do each step as well as I can. I need to see Corey, to be able to touch him, to let him touch me if he needs to.

It's still light, probably about eight-thirty, but feels earlier because of its being close to the summer solstice. So, up Bonnie's driveway I go, one foot in front of the other. I don't feel like I'm going home, and that's kind of a relief because if I did, I would also have to feel wrong for leaving. The Mercedes isn't here. What if they're not home? I wonder if the key is still hidden under the potted plant on the deck. What if I have to wait? Should I go in, or go back to Natalie's? If I go inside and fall asleep, and they come home and find me, it will be worse than facing them at the door. What if they're gone for the holiday and don't come home until tomorrow night?

I'm on the porch now. The house is dark. The porch light is off, a sign that they're not away for the weekend. They leave it on when they're gone. I push the button and hear the bell chime its annoying little tune. It's quiet. I wait. Then I hear the creaking sounds of movement behind the door. It opens.

Bonnie looks like she's been sleeping. She does that, falls asleep in her recliner downstairs in front of the TV. Our eyes meet. I feel the shock as she registers that it's me. Her eyes break from mine and she turns aside. She lets out a wail, an animal sound that would have cut straight through me even if I didn't know I was the one who caused it.

It brings up the image of the cement bathtub/coffin from Emily's poem. The sound that comes from Bonnie is the way you'd feel if the ice water was gushing from everywhere and you were too helpless and burning-cold-frozen to cry out, except you'd have to because you couldn't bear it any other way. It's the wail you would let out because the pain is overwhelming and you know there's no fixing it or getting away from it, and the only relief from it is in releasing the anguish. It's a horrible sound and I hope I never hear it again.

She bends over like her stomach has cramped, or her heart, and she needs to catch her breath or is going to throw up. My eyes well up immediately. I feel helpless and responsible and I'm crying hard again. All I can think to do is put my arm over her shoulder and say, "I'm sorry," because I'm sorry for both of us, separately and together.

I hold on tight with my arm and don't let go until she pulls herself together enough to face me, and I hug her until she finally hugs me back and I realize that the valves go both ways, whether you're paying attention or not, and that from this moment on I can't be a kid anymore about the cold water I let my valves release.

"They had divers looking for your body in the river. Where have you been? Why?"

So here it is. My big chance to explain. Sterling, if he's here, isn't showing himself. For this moment, she's all mine and I don't know where to start, so I dig into my pack that has somehow gotten from my back to the floor of the porch, and come up with the birth certificate. I hand it to her. "Who am I? Kristen or Amy? I'll tell you where I've been when I know who I am." I say it matter-of-factly, trying not to be challenging or insolent. She looks at it only long enough to recognize it, then says, "Oh my God! How did you get this?"

"I was borrowing some earrings. It was under the jewelry box. I didn't go looking for it."

She's crying. She takes my hand and leads me to the kitchen where she takes down two wine glasses and pours the expensive red wine she drinks, a full glass for herself and half a glass for me. We sit silently at the table for a long time.

She finally says, "I'm not very good at this so it will be hard for me. I'm glad Sterling isn't here. He had work in Seattle today that's keeping him late. He'll be home in the morning. Amy was your sister."

"I have a sister? Why didn't you tell me?"

"I guess it was easier to keep it buried. It's a hard memory. I gave you her middle name after she died."

"So I really am Kristen? Is my last name Mackenzie or Nichols? Am I Canadian or American?"

"Technically, you're a Mackenzie. Sterling never legally adopted you. But I've been with him since before you started school and your having a different name would have required a lot of explanation I didn't want to give, so I had it changed when you were still small. You have dual citizenship. Your father was Canadian, but you were born in Seattle."

"Is my father alive?"

"No."

"How did he die?" I locked in on her eyes. I could tell she didn't want to answer. So I pleaded, "I need to know, Bonnie." The "Bonnie," just slipped out. "I have to know who I am."

"Bonnie?"

"Yes. Bonnie. It doesn't feel right to call you Mom. I've been thinking of you as Bonnie for years. The most important thing I learned from going away, and the reason I came back, is that pretending doesn't work. It makes you crazy, and I'm not going to pretend anymore. I don't want you to either, at least not with me."

She doesn't say anything, but just looks at me, like maybe I am a ghost after all, or she's having a bad dream.

"Do you want to know why I left?"

She is quiet, but she's listening.

"I left because leaving wasn't permanent. I walked around all the time feeling like making that sound you just made. My whole life has been a lie for years, and I just couldn't do it anymore. I hate Sterling. He's a greedy hypocrite. I hate church. God doesn't go there. School's okay. At least some of it is about important things, but for me it isn't about the high-paying career everyone says is so important. It's about knowing the truth. And I want to know the truth about my father.

"I wrote you a letter to let you know I wasn't dead, but it didn't get here and I'm sorry for letting you think I was dead. I left because when you leave, you can come back. I didn't commit suicide. I went away to see if I could live on my own, and if not living the lie I had to live in order to stay in this house would make me like living. I didn't starve, and I didn't cut myself once while I was gone. It wasn't all fun. Some of it was scary, but I learned I could make it on my own. Because I was a runaway, I was still living a lie, a different lie, so I came back. I'm here and I'm through pretending, and I'm not afraid to leave again if that's what I have to do."

There's a long silence before she says, "I don't know if it was an accident or suicide, but your father died of a drug overdose. He changed when Amy died. You were about a year old when it happened. By then you girls slept in your own room, but hadn't been doing it for long. After your sister died, I was afraid something would happen to you and we put your crib in our room. At night you'd wake and cry because you weren't used to being without Amy. I was walking with you, singing to you just before I found him. I sang "Old Man River," and "Hush, Little Baby," because those were the songs whose words I knew.

"When I got you back to sleep, I went to the kitchen for a glass of water. He was on the couch. At first, I thought he was asleep and I went over to get him to go to bed. It was a weeknight and he had to work in the morning. He was a pipefitter and worked a lot of overtime. Except for our grief over Amy, I thought we had a good life. He made enough money so that I didn't have to work; I could stay home with you. We lived well and I had no suspicion of the drugs. Even then I tended to see only what I wanted to be true.

"I sensed something even before my foot bumped against the syringe on the carpet. His position was wrong. You couldn't be comfortable, sleeping like that. He was on his back, one arm draped over the back of the couch and one foot on the floor, but his back was too high up on the armrest. As I moved toward him, I saw the light from the street lamp outside reflecting off his eyes.

His mouth was open. Even as I was screaming at him, shaking
him, trying to wake him up, I knew he was dead. But I couldn't
accept it. Maybe I still haven't accepted it. Maybe I'm still mad at
him for doing it.

"You would have liked him, or at least the part of him I knew
and was in love with. We had a good life until your sister died.
I know I was happy and I have to believe he was too, and that
her death is what changed him. We were married right after I
graduated from high school. He was older but only by three years,
so he was twenty-one when I graduated. He had dual citizenship.
His parents lived in Vancouver but had lived down here when he
was born. Amy was born in Vancouver. We didn't have medical
insurance and health care there is free."

I watched Bonnie's face. As she told me how she met my
father, it was more alive than I'd ever seen it. They met on the
Fourth of July at Gasworks Park in Seattle, where they'd gone to
watch the fireworks. Her friends were flirting with him and his
buddies, but he picked her out to talk to. Tomorrow would be a
kind of anniversary for them.

"How did Amy die?" I asked.

"A truck hit her. She was his angel. It should have been a
normal day. I was cooking dinner and needed butter. There was a
market nearby and he took her along. When they left, he had her
on his shoulders, but she could get squirmy. On the way back he
had groceries, and when he stopped to talk to a neighbor, he set
her down. For a second, he wasn't watching. She saw a squirrel
under a tree across the street and darted out between two cars
just as the truck came around the corner. He couldn't forgive
himself."

"God, Mom, that's awful. Then he died and left you alone
with me. I'm sorry."

"So I'm your mom again?" There was a hint of bitterness in
her voice.

"Well, I guess. I mean, I can sort of understand. I know I had another stepdad before. At least Sterling's predictable. He's a jerk, but you know he's not going to kill himself."

"Sterling has been very good to us."

"Wait until he finds out that I only ran away and I'm not dead, that I wasn't murdered. As soon as the shock wears off, he's not going to be nice to me."

"He just has high expectations of people. He's not that bad."

"So what was my other stepdad like?"

"At first he was nice, but he was a mistake. I think I was so hurt and scared that my judgment was bad. I didn't really love him, not like I loved your dad. I had never had a job and I was alone with a baby. He took care of us when I was feeling helpless."

"Why'd you guys split up?"

"It's complicated. There were a lot of reasons. I don't really want to talk about it. I didn't think he was good for you, and I didn't love him."

"Do you love Sterling?"

"I'm fond of him. He's taken good care of us."

"What would make you leave him?"

"I'm not going to answer that. I thought you had a right to know about your father, so I told you. Maybe if I had told you sooner, we could have avoided all this. I'm sorry you don't like Sterling, but he is my husband. Thinking you'd been killed has been very hard on him, on both of us. This will be a big shock for him and I'm glad we had some time by ourselves first.

"Now I want to hear about you, where you went and how you lived. We also need to let the police know. They think that Corey boy killed you."

So I told her about going to Victoria, about being a waitress, and about the letter that never arrived. I left out the part about Grant and being stalked. She did want to know whether I had boyfriends there, which I took to mean was I still a virgin, which,

strange as it may seem, I am. She knew about me going out to
Corey's campsite on the river and told me about the blood they
found on my sock there and finding my hair on his fleece, which
made me feel responsible and horrible and I wanted to call him
right away, but by then it was really late and I didn't.

Finally she said we should go to bed. She said we needed
to call the police in the morning. I hugged her and said, "Good
night, Mom. You've had enough hurt in your life. Maybe I sensed
it all those years that I tried to be the perfect kid. I was afraid
something awful would happen if I made the slightest slip-up,
but something had to change. I'm sorry I caused you more pain."

She hugged me back and said, "I should have told you a long
time ago, but I tend to see what I want to, and your life seemed
to be going so well. You're alive and you're back. That's the
important thing. No one died. We'll get through this. I'm sorry
too, Kristen. I'm glad I'm your mom again."

My bedroom was exactly the way I had left it, stuffed animals
and all. I shoved them all in a pile on the floor before I climbed
into bed.

Kristen

The noise that drew me back from my dark, dead-to-the-world, dreamless sleep was loud and sharp, like a cupboard door slamming or something being smacked down hard on a tabletop.

"It was completely selfish! That's what it was. She's a self-centered little tramp!"

It took a second to understand. I thought I was having a nightmare until I saw the stuffed animals on the floor and remembered that I was in my old room in Sterling's house, and Sterling was home.

"It doesn't matter why she did it! I don't care what she thought. There is simply no reason that could justify doing what she did. She put this whole valley through hell."

Sterling's house is on a hillside overlooking Skagit Bay and Goat Island. It's a nice house. My room is on the lower floor and has a view. The window opens wide enough to climb through, but there is a screen on the outside. You can remove the screen by lifting up and pushing the bottom out. I had to be careful not to let it fall. I was glad I had brought my backpack into my room, and I dropped it to the ground first. Then I was out. I pulled the window shut and replaced the screen before I snuck around the side of the house and out to the street. I had also made the bed and put the stuffed animals back on it. Maybe it was my way of trying to change reality back into a nightmare I could wake up from.

I wanted my bike. I had to find Corey. I had a phone number Natalie gave me, but didn't have an address or a phone to make the call. He walked and hitched everywhere, or took the SKAT bus. It was the morning of the Fourth of July, a little after eleven. I thought Sterling might have called the detective's cell phone, but if he knew I had left again, he might wait. He would be thinking about how it would look, and it might be embarrassing to tell them I had come home but was gone again, and they didn't know where I was.

If they came looking, it would be hard for me to hide. I didn't know where to go. If Trish was home, she would let me in even if Natalie was at work, but I didn't want to cause her trouble; Sterling and Bonnie would know to look there. The best thing was to go to the cops myself. I got out the bus schedule and saw that I could get a bus to Mount Vernon outside the Shelter Bay gate at 12:30. So that's where I headed. Then I thought that because it was a holiday, the office was probably closed. To get a cop, you'd have to call 911 or have someone's off-duty number. So I decided to use Trish's phone.

I made it outside the Shelter Bay gate just by walking down the side of the road like it was a normal day. There were people in their yards, and cars went by. Some kids from school drove past. They looked at me a little funny, but didn't stop. It felt weird to be back from the dead. When I was past the guard shack and near the corner of Natalie's street, I still had half an hour before the bus came. I figured if Trish wasn't home, I would come back.

Then I saw one of the reservation cop cars parked at the entrance to the village. They look like State Patrol cruisers, and sometimes they set up a trap there to catch speeders. Instead of going to Natalie's, I walked over to it. The window was open and the guy looked at me over his radar gun, which was pointed toward the bend where cars came after crossing the bridge. He seemed intent on what he was doing but nodded politely, like he expected me to ask for directions or something.

"I need to talk to you," I said. That got him to really look at me.

"Okay. I'm listening."

"My name is Kristen Nichols and I think everyone thinks I'm dead, but I'm not."

The tribe's police station was just down the street, and he was apologetic about it, but made me ride in the caged-in back seat. He took my pack and put it in the trunk, but didn't frisk me. He asked if I had talked to my parents, and I told him I had and that my stepdad was pretty mad and was part of the reason I left in the first place, so I didn't feel comfortable staying there. The offices were empty and he had me sit down and wait while he called Bonnie. Then he called a sheriff's detective, the one whose card Bonnie had.

Bonnie came without Sterling. It's funny, but as soon as I heard Sterling's voice yelling earlier, she became Bonnie again in my head, instead of Mom. Eventually the detective showed up. It was a long afternoon. He seemed almost disappointed that I was back and wanted to know every detail about the night I went out to Corey's campsite, and the night I left and how I got from the car to the ferry dock, and why I left. I was as honest as I could be, but didn't rat out Natalie's neighbor. Bonnie was really supportive, which was a nice surprise. It helped make our talk last night feel real.

I told the detective I wanted to see Corey, that he was my friend. I needed to tell him I was sorry. I was insistent, but he said I should wait. He said seeing him right away wouldn't be a good idea, because he'd been through a lot and could be unstable. The detective said he would tell Corey I was back.

Finally, he said there could be charges brought against me, but they would have to review the case with the prosecutor's office. For now, since I was under eighteen, they would release me to my mom. It was absolutely imperative that she know where I was at all times. If I couldn't agree to that, I would have to go to the detention center.

I agreed and went home with her. She was quiet, but did say that Sterling had calmed down a little and was trying to make the best of it. I took that to mean that he had already figured out what the detective had told us. The newspapers and TV stations would find out soon that I was back and reporters would want to talk to us. Sterling knew it would be best for him if we looked like a family reconciling our problems, reaching for a happy ending, so publicly he would act as if that was true.

I would be a prisoner in my room, living out the reality that I thought was a nightmare when I woke up to it this morning. But there was one big difference. Bonnie was stepping out from behind Sterling, trying to be my mom, and I thought he'd do his best to stay away from me. I'll make that as easy for him as I can.

As soon as I can get alone with a telephone, I'm calling Corey.

Corey

My dad was watching TV, his bottomless evening drink in hand, when the phone rang. I was in my room listening to music. The phone doesn't ring all that much and I didn't even hear it. It's never for me. He brought it in, so I took off my headphones.

It was my mom. I was surprised to hear her voice. I hadn't seen her since that day she came to visit when I was in Juvie, so it was pretty awkward having her on the other end of the phone. After the hello, the only thing I could think to say was, "So why are you calling?'

"Corey, I feel like I haven't handled this very well. I believe you didn't do it. It's time to move on with our lives. Tristan keeps asking about you. She misses you. Since tomorrow is the Fourth of July, and Harold isn't here—he'll be gone for the rest of the week—I thought you could come over for dinner. We can barbeque a chicken and then the three of us can walk over the hill and watch the fireworks."

Tristan is really cute and really smart. I think I pushed her out of my mind during all of this because it mattered to me what she thought, and I didn't want to know if she was angry with me. It felt good to hear that she'd been asking about me though, and I wondered what they'd told her. It's not her fault Harold is her dad any more than it's my fault he's my stepdad, or that my dad is the way he is.

"Do you really want to walk downtown with me?"

"Corey, I'm trying to say I'm sorry. Please come. I can pick you up tomorrow afternoon."

So here I am. It's the first time I've been in this town since the police hauled me away the morning after Kristen disappeared. It feels surreal. I guess that's the right word. Kind of dreamy, like I'm stoned and not sure what to trust, only I'm not stoned, which makes it a little spooky. Everything looks the same. I don't know if you've ever lived in a small town, but here everyone knows everything about everyone else. In one way though, I think this place is unusual for a small town. Maybe because the reservation is so close, people have had to learn to accept difference. I mean people do things that, somewhere else, would make other people drive them away, but here they just keep on living their lives. But if they think you hurt someone, one of the family, I'm not sure they forgive so easily, so I was more than a little nervous.

I'm pushing Tristan on the swing while my mom is cooking inside. My mom makes this dynamite chicken that she has to come out and baste continually with this vinegar-and-egg sauce. It gets really smoky and good. So I'm pushing Tristan and she likes it and wants to go higher. Then, out of the blue, she makes me stop the swing and looks at me all earnest and puzzled.

"Corey, why did you go away?"

How do you explain it to a five year old? I said, "You know how your dad isn't really my dad, and I have another dad?"

"Yes."

"Well, my dad missed me, so I'm giving him a turn."

"My dad says you were in jail and that you did something bad."

"It wasn't really jail, and they made a mistake."

"My dad says what you did was really bad."

"I didn't do it though. Something really bad happened to someone. That part is probably true. They needed to find the mean person who did it so that everyone would be safe again. Because I get in trouble at school sometimes, they thought it might be me, but it wasn't, so they let me come home to my real dad's house. Did you miss me?"

"Yes."

"I missed you too."

My mom makes really good potato salad too, and the chicken and the salad were the best food I'd had since before all this started. After we ate, the three of us watched one of Tristan's kid movies to pass the time. The poison seemed gone from the air and it felt good, just sitting on the couch with them, the best I'd felt in months. When the light outside started to fade, we got some blankets and those lightweight, folding yard chairs. I was holding Tristan's hand and had her special little chair along with a normal-size one for me tucked under my other arm. We were on the front yard sidewalk, just about out to the street, when Harold's pickup comes roaring up. I knew by the way he got out that he had stopped somewhere and tipped a few. I could tell my mom was really surprised.

"I didn't expect to see you until Saturday," she said.

"The boat blew a reduction gear. I'm off for a day or two. What's the little pervert doing here?"

He didn't even slow down but came right up to me and grabbed me by the shirt.

"Stay away from my daughter, you little worm."

He had the sweatshirt and the windbreaker I was wearing all wadded up in his big hammy paws. Like I said earlier, he's pretty big. He lifted me off the ground. I dropped the chairs and let go of Tristan's hand. She was yelling, "Daddy, Daddy, don't hurt Corey," and was grabbing at his leg.

He threw me and I landed on my butt on the lawn. Tristan ran towards me and Harold grabbed her and picked her up. My mom was crying.

"I hurried home so I could watch the fireworks with my family, and you're not going to wreck that too, you little shit. You're nothing but trouble."

He picked up the chairs I'd dropped. "We're going and you're leaving. You goddamned well better not be here when we get back or I'll take care of you myself. Keep your perverted ass away from my daughter or you're dead meat."

He grabbed my mom by the arm and pushed her down the sidewalk. Both she and Tristan were quiet as they headed up the street. I sat there wet-eyed for a minute, so crazy mad and sad I couldn't move. Then I got up and went in the house. I went straight for Harold's MacNaughtons and slugged down a pretty good hit. The burning felt good in my mouth and throat. I took the bottle into their bedroom and sat on the bed, his side. I took another slug, then opened the nightstand drawer. It was right there, out in the open where I knew it would be, lying on top of his socks, a fucking .44 magnum cannon. I picked it up. It was loaded.

I sat holding it, looking at it. I looked down the barrel for a long time. I took one more little hit from the bottle and put the gun in the pouch of the hooded sweatshirt I was wearing under my windbreaker. I closed the drawer and put the bottle back in the cupboard, then left. The big fireworks hadn't started yet, but the whistling of rockets and popping of firecrackers and the occasional M-80 booms had started coming from the rez. The gun weighed a ton and would have been noticeable in the daylight, but it was twilight, and in any case, I didn't care.

I walked up past the Catholic church. There were other people headed the same way. I figured Harold would go down by the boat launch. The view from there is good and there are places to put the chairs, but it's not as crowded as closer in and he probably wasn't in the mood to be social, though I'd seen him throw the switch in a second when he needed to.

I decided to go down by Maple Hall first. There's space for parking there too, and more good spots for chairs. It got pretty crowded as I neared the water. Any open spot with the view not blocked by buildings had people standing or sitting in it, but I didn't see Harold. I headed toward the boat launch, winding between the parked cars and people, the weight of the gun bouncing against my belly.

I felt a hand on my arm, and heard a girl's voice saying urgently, "Corey, Corey!" I turned and that's when it got really surreal. She looked different, but I recognized her. I didn't believe it was really happening. I mean I was pretty much over the edge already, in that crazy place where nothing matters anymore. I had the bomb strapped to me, so to speak, and something was going to happen. Then there's this ghost pulling on me, saying my name. She pulled me around to face her, her hands on my arms. She was desperate too, and her eyes were wet.

"Corey, Corey. I'm sorry. I'm so sorry. I had no idea they would do that to you."

Then she took both my hands in hers. They felt warm, the way Tristan's feel. I could barely say her name.

"Kristen."

"It's me, Corey. I'm back. I spent the day with that detective. He said he would tell you. I called your dad's house before we came into town, but you weren't there. I'm so sorry for what they did to you."

I'm still dazed, trying to take it in. Our hands are between us. She's holding tight, waiting for a reaction, waiting for me to say something, which I can't do yet because it's as if my brain has short-circuited, and I don't know whether to laugh or cry or just collapse on the ground. Then one of her hands brushes the gun.

"Is that for me?"

It hits me that she's real and what it means, and my knees are all jelly and my throat is tight and I really am about to pop, only in an entirely different way than it would have been before she appeared, and the gun has nothing to do with anything any more but I can't make my mouth work to tell her because it's taking everything I have to hold in this crying thing that's about to happen, but I can't let it out here in public.

"It's okay if it is. I can't undo what they did to you and it's my fault for running away. But you should know before you do it that I used your story about your uncle and Hawaii, and that I did try to let people know I wasn't dead. I sent a letter. But I remembered how your uncle got caught. I didn't go to Hawaii but tried to have the letter mailed from there. But it didn't come, and I screwed up and ended up hurting people. Hurting you."

"You ran away?"

"To Victoria. I worked as a waitress."

So instead of crying or collapsing or blowing Harold's head off, or my head off in front of Harold, or shooting her like she thought I was going to, all that shit came out of me in something that sounded like laughter. I was crying at the same time, of course, the first real tears since the night I woke up and knew my mom was in that tent with Harold back when I was ten, but because the fireworks had started and the sky was full of red, white, blue, and green explosions, I don't think anyone but Kristen heard it, and if it scared her, she took it pretty well. She hung on tight to my hands and shared the ride. There was real insanity in it, desperation, but her hands stayed connected to mine, and a lot of poison came out, and in the end, the absurdity was too good and the laughter won.

"Boy, am I glad to see you," was what I said when I could make words.

She looked at me for a long time.

"Are you sure?"

"The gun was for Harold, or me."

"Oh Jesus!"

"I'll be okay now. They were clueless here. I mean totally clueless. What made you come back?"

So she told me a little bit about it, and about the night she left here, and about how now she was pretty much restricted until the prosecutor decided how much trouble she was in. We didn't have enough time because her mom was hovering not far away, watching us, so we agreed to talk again as soon as she could make it happen. She said her mom was being pretty cool about it all, but her stepdad wasn't. Then she hugged me and left. The gun felt huge between us and she made me promise not to do anything stupid, which I did, promise I mean, and I hurried back to Harold's house, hoping I would have time to put it back and be gone before they got home.

It didn't happen that way, and though her trust hung heavy on me I did something I have always wanted to do.

The lights were on and I could see my mom and Harold at the kitchen table. Harold had a beer and was talking, gesturing, like he was lecturing her. I had to get the gun back to him or he would accuse me of stealing it. I didn't need any more trouble. I snuck up to the window to get a better look, and watched them for a while, making sure Tristan was in bed, deciding what to do next. First, I emptied the bullets out of the gun. I had to do it right. I didn't want any accidents.

I put the bullets in my pocket and had the gun in my hand when I walked in the door. I went straight to the kitchen. The gun was clearly visible, and menacing with the safety off, but it was pointed at the ground. His eyes bugged when he saw it, and the expression was pretty close to the way I'd imagined it would be. He started to say something, but I stopped him.

"Shut up, asshole, and listen for once in your life.

"You called me a pervert in front of my sister and my mom. You threatened to kill me. I'm not a pervert. I'm not a murderer, and I don't have to take that kind of shit from you or anyone else anymore."

I could see real fear in his eyes, and I let it soak in for a minute before saying,

"Kristen's back. Nobody killed her. She ran away. Her stepdad's an asshole too. It will all be in the paper tomorrow."

I let that soak in for a minute, then said, "You're a fucking idiot and you don't deserve to own this. You shouldn't threaten innocent people and you shouldn't leave loaded weapons lying around where kids can find them."

I set the gun on the table and dropped the handful of bullets in a potted plant as I walked out the door. I didn't know how I would get back to my dad's, so I started walking. It's more than ten miles and I was debating whether to risk trying to hitch a ride. The newspaper hadn't declared me innocent yet, and Harold isn't the only nutcase in the Valley. I hadn't gone far and was still shaky when my mom pulled up.

"Get in," she said. "I invited you here, and I'm giving you a ride back, whether he likes it or not."

Kristen

It's amazing, but I don't think Corey hates me or blames me for what happened to him. He sure scared the crap out of me though. I couldn't stop worrying until I talked to him on the phone the next day. Letting him know I'm back was maybe the most intense thing I've ever done, and lately my life has had its intense moments. It's strange how some things just fall into place and others don't. I could easily have not been there, or not seen him, and he could have gone and done whatever he was going to do with that gun.

But he didn't. The next day when I heard his voice on the phone all calm and normal, it made me wonder. We were there in the dark with the sky lit up and rockets whistling and exploding, and him feeling crazy with that gun, and me afraid that what I did would cause him to break. Then, when he finally understood that it really was me, that I wasn't dead, but had chosen to do what I did, there we were, all normal, talking on the phone the next day. I had to wonder which parts were real and which were a dream. And I had to wonder why we were able to escape from the abyss when lots of people aren't. All it takes is an icy road and a telephone pole to make a simple trip home from a friend's house become a tragedy. It happened to a kid at our school last year, yet somehow we seem to be sliding through all this.

So what Corey ended up doing with the gun was actually pretty funny. He told me how he returned it, and about how he used to imagine having bombs strapped to him, which sounds pretty dramatic, but I get it. It's like everyone gets wound up in their own agenda and other people get overlooked or pushed away. I don't think Corey's mom was trying to hurt him when she got with Harold, or my dad was trying to hurt me when he overdosed. I know I wasn't trying to hurt Corey or my mom when I ran away. I just hurt inside. I was desperate and had to do something. In a way, what Corey was imagining with the bomb belt was like me standing up to Grant. I had to be willing to risk it all, or it would just keep going along the way it was.

Bonnie is letting me use the Taurus sometimes now. We talk quite a bit, and she trusts me. It feels pretty good, like we're finally connecting. She's standing up to Sterling, too. I don't think that would have happened if I hadn't left. I heard them yelling the other night, probably about me, and she threatened to move out. She started looking for a new job the next day and told me we might be poor soon, so I should enjoy our comfort while we have it. She seems happier. I know I am, but Sterling probably isn't. Sometimes you need a big jolt to face the truth.

They didn't charge me with anything, which is a relief. I guess I didn't break any major laws. I didn't steal the car. I did take some of Sterling's money, but he gave me the debit card and the PIN to use in an emergency, so he would have to bring charges and he would look pretty dumb. The letter from Hawaii finally got here. It helped, even if it was three months late and not from Hawaii. It showed up in Natalie's mailbox, sealed in a bigger envelope with Canadian postage on it. There was a note inside from Trudy's friend saying she forgot to mail it in Hawaii.

I skipped school for two months. They could have a court hearing on that if the school makes an issue of it, but they won't because I'm a good student and they have bigger problems to spend their time on. Now that Corey seems okay, school may be my biggest real problem. I'm short of credits for graduation. I missed half a semester, which means I don't have passing grades in any of my classes. If the teachers would let me, I could make it up, but I doubt that all of them will. This isn't like having cancer, or being injured in a car wreck, or even having mono, though they let a girl who had been drinking and got hurt when she ran her car off the road make up her work. As Sterling likes to remind mom, it was my fault, and there has to be consequences, so we shouldn't expect any help from him to pay for my college, if I can even get in now.

It's been a week since the fireworks. Bonnie let me have the Taurus for a night out. I think she knows I'll see Corey tonight and probably accepts it. He's definitely not her idea of good boyfriend material, but she knows I have a connection to him. I'm finding out that Mom's pretty human when you find your way to her. So I park the Taurus in front of Corey's dad's house in Burlington. The neighborhood has a similar feel to the one where Natalie lives—kind of decayed, but in a different way—and the house is grimy inside, like Ian's uncle's house in Victoria when I moved in.

Corey shows me his room, which is a guy room and kind of messy. Then he says, "This place is depressing. I don't want to hang around here unless you do. We could go for a walk, only the neighborhood is depressing too. I haven't been out to the campsite since the night they took me to Juvie. We could go out there and build a fire."

So we went. It was early and would stay light for hours. We stopped at the market and got some hot dogs and buns and chips. He had a pack all ready, with everything else we needed in it, which didn't surprise me. There's a road over the dike and a place to park on the river side, out of view from the road, but we didn't care who saw us. Our story had been in the papers and even made the Seattle TV news. I was kind of the villain now and he was the victim, but we didn't think anyone would bother us.

As we walked in, I remembered what it felt like to walk that trail in the dark that other night, and how alone I felt then, and how I trusted Corey because I thought he knew more about aloneness than I did, and that he respected me. I still think that. So I took his hand, just like I did that night, and we carried our picnic stuff to the river. The rock-circle fire pit was still there and, at first, the place had a weird feel to it. There were bits of colored plastic, numbered in black marker, tied to branches, and a stillness, an emptiness, like no one had used it since my tragic death. We built a fire.

He told me what it was like that last night, and about the fight with Harold that made him decide to sleep there and about hoping I would drive by and pick him up when he was walking. He wouldn't talk about Juvie, so I told him about leaving the car and about Natalie's neighbor giving me a ride and me hoping that he didn't recognize me, and about all the strange moments that could easily have gone differently and made me turn back, but didn't, like passing through Customs and finding a place to stay and a job. Then I told him again how really sorry I was.

And he kissed me.

And I kissed him back.

Corey

I had it all planned. I didn't know if she would go, but she went out there with me to the river. It was strange, driving up, parking the car, walking down the trail, holding her hand. But it felt good too. The cops hadn't cleaned up after themselves. I pulled down as many of their little plastic flags as I could. Once we got the fire going, I cut some sticks for the hot dogs and loosened up a little.

The river felt alive, the current rippling, the surface moving and changing in the reflected sunlight. There was a kingfisher working an eddy on the other side, hovering above it in that distinct, fluttery way, then dropping hard with a splash and coming up again and flying to a limb to rest and eat. There's a myth about kingfishers. They mate for life, and when this ancient Greek lady's husband got killed in a shipwreck, the gods turned her into a kingfisher and brought him back to life as one too, in honor of their deep love for each other. I asked Kristen if she remembered the story and she didn't, but she wasn't in that class with me. Maybe the reason I remembered it was because of the husband's name. It was Ceyx, and we made jokes in class by pronouncing it "sex."

Then she told me how sorry she was about them blaming me for killing her and I kissed her.

Maybe I would have blamed her if things had turned out differently. If I had just seen her there with her mom when I was looking for Harold, I don't know what I would have done. I was pretty much over the edge, and the surprise might have had a different effect. But she came to me, touched me and apologized. Her need for my forgiveness was part of the package, part of what I had to take in with the fact of her presence, the end of her absence.

There was nothing fake about it. She wouldn't let go of my hands, like she really wanted to understand the place I was in and be connected to it, even if it was dangerous, which it was. She was willing to come out to the edge with me. And I remembered the trust I felt in her hands, walking out here that other night. And she had pulled off the vanishing act, like my uncle, only smarter and better, which made me an accomplice, a partner in something I thought you could only dream about. So instead of being tragic, something I could feel sorry for myself about, them blaming me became funny and absurd because the whole thing is funny and absurd. And tragic. But in the end more funny and absurd than tragic.

And she kissed me back.

She trusted me. What happened that night, or didn't, would become part of my baggage, one of the things I carry with me, like Smith offering me his boat money, believing in me when no one else did. It has become part of my truth now, something I have to live up to. Now someone else I care about, trust and respect, believes that I'm worthy of her trust and respect, so I have to live up to it too. It's pretty heavy stuff.

So if we did it, had sex, it means I took on the responsibility for being enough of a man to be worthy of her, and if I can't do that, if I'm not ready to do that, I'm a loser. If we didn't do it, maybe I passed up my big chance. Or, maybe I saved myself from becoming a loser. I will say this. She makes me want to be worthy of her friendship. That connection, the one that involves trust and honesty, is what's most important. It's new to me and I don't want to lose it.

What happened is private.

Natalie

The strangest thing about the last six months is how it seems to have just faded away. The trauma and intensity just flattened out like it would after a near-miss car crash, except that it got stretched out over a longer period of time. Of course it's left its marks on all of us. A lot of important things are different from what they would have been if Kristen had just obeyed her curfew that night and stayed home and done whatever Sterling and Bonnie wanted her to do, pretending to be happy, going to school and doing her homework, living in that room full of stuffed animals. They're gone now, the stuffed animals. We took them to the Salvation Army store instead of the dump, so maybe some kid will give them a chance at another life.

Christmas has come and gone. Brad and I are a real couple now. I did some family stuff with him at Christmas. His mom is still pretty icy, but as far as I know she hasn't disowned him yet. I got accepted at Wazoo—you know, Washington State University in Pullman—which is where Brad is going. I would rather have gone to the University of Washington in Seattle, but Brad's family has a Cougar tradition, and for him, Seattle is too close to home anyway. Wazoo is a party school. It's so far out in the sticks, there's nothing else to do, but just going to a real university instead of a community college is a huge step for me, so I'm not too particular which one. I got a good financial aid package, but the main thing is that Brad will be there.

When school started this fall, I didn't know what to expect.

I assumed there would be a lot of drama about Kristen running away, that some people would be really mad at her. Some of the teachers are chilly toward her. Some people are big on accountability and punishment, and seem to think they have to create consequences above and beyond the natural ones. Like the reward they get for being good isn't worth much unless bad people suffer. As if life doesn't create its own version of hell. I think being good brings its own rewards; they're just not always immediate. I think if she tried hard enough, Kristen could have gotten the school to force those teachers to let her make up the work. They do it all the time, but she decided she wants to do Running Start.

She takes classes at Skagit Valley Community College, and the high school has to pay the tuition. The high school is pretty anal about graduation requirements. They think they're pretty special. They have the highest credit requirement in the valley and won't accept substitutions for certain classes like English and history, even if you took those classes at the college. Kristen has plenty of credits to get her diploma through the college, and the only drawback is she wouldn't get to suit up and walk with her class at graduation. Her grade point average is good and she got accepted at some good colleges.

But she might not be able to go because of money, which is really tragic. Because she ran away, Sterling won't pay for her college. But because he makes as much money as he does, she doesn't qualify for financial aid. She says she's moving to Seattle after graduation, no matter what, even if it means she can only go to school part time. Their house is pretty crazy now. Sometimes it's like a war zone and sometimes Sterling is all nice. Bonnie quit working in Sterling's office and now works at a bank. She doesn't make as much, but for now it doesn't matter because Sterling has plenty. But Kristen says she and Bonnie might move out, which would solve her school problems. Since Sterling didn't adopt her, they would be poor enough for financial aid. It's a weird world.

So she's taking classes both at the high school and at the community college. She got to play soccer with us, and she's at school enough that I see her nearly every day. We're even better friends than before she went to Victoria. Only now we're not like opposites. Sometimes I miss being the strong one, but we have a lot more in common. We even look alike. People joke about it.

To some, she's kind of a hero now. I mean, what kid hasn't thought about running away, but she pulled it off, like Huck Finn. She didn't come back all beat either, or full of rebellion and bravado. She's playing it straight. When kids ask her, she just says parts of it were fun and parts of it were hard. No bullshit from her. She's worked hard in her classes, and though she's nice about it, she gets really impatient when immature kids waste class time.

In spite of what people think about kids and of the way we act sometimes, we really do know we have to grow up. A lot of kids just haven't been jolted much by reality. Adults protect them, and so much of what we get from adults is laced with bullshit. It makes it easy to pretend the important stuff doesn't apply to us. What's true is that most adults haven't figured out good answers to the important stuff either.

But they pretend they know, pretend there are simple answers, like if you obey your parents, get good grades, and go to college, you'll have a happy, successful life. What they really mean is that if you listen to them, you might improve your odds a little, and then their lives will be easier. We're not idiots; we listen to and watch them, and we try to manipulate them the same way they try to manipulate their circumstances. The world is a messy place. Life is risky, full of uncertainties, disappointments, disasters, and just plain noise.

The best we can do is weed out the bull and try not to add any. My parents are losers, but I have something a lot of kids don't have. Trish plays it straight with me, and she loves me. That's huge. Brad and I are still playing it straight. I don't know about that kind of love yet. What we have might last and it might not, but for now I'm going with it in spite of his mother. Brad may eventually have to choose, or his mother may have to soften. Or we might just drift apart.

Oh, I almost forgot to tell you about Kristen and Corey. I have to admit I still have a hard time with Corey, but I don't hate him anymore. It's hard to forgive. Even though she hasn't said it, I know that's what Kristen wants me to do. Corey seems to have forgiven her, which I don't completely understand. If it wasn't for already having a date with Brad, I would have helped egg Corey's house. I probably would have helped lynch him if the circumstances had been right. I know he was screwed because of what she did, really screwed, but within a week or two after she got back, they were like good friends. It made me jealous. They're not a couple exactly, but they have some understanding, almost like they're co-conspirators. It's an odd relationship. I haven't tried to get her to explain it to me, but eventually I will.

He wrote me this letter. It was a card actually, and pretty short. He brought it to my house with a flower, a white rose. He just handed it to me and left. He apologized for the camera thing. He said he was a dumb kid, but it was still an asshole thing to do, and he wishes he could take it back, but he can't, so he's sorry. I'm sure Kristen put him up to it, and at first I was mad. But after I thought about it, I decided that maybe it's okay. She's my friend and they're good friends. It's not like I can just forgive and forget all at once, but my attitude is changing.

He's going to this alternative school in Mount Vernon and will graduate at the same time we do. He came to some of Kristen's and my soccer games, and some football and basketball games too. People seem to accept him now. He and Kristen talk on the phone a lot. Even I can tell he's changed. He has a job now, washing dishes at a restaurant near his dad's house, so he doesn't have much free time. She says he's saving money so he can get out of the Valley.

Oh yeah. I got my car. It's a blue Mazda Protégé, not even close to new, but no big dents or torn seats. These old people had it before me and they took good care of it. Sometimes, when Sterling is on a rampage and won't let her have the Taurus because he paid for it even if it is in Bonnie's name, I let Kristen drive my car. She bought a bike and sometimes last fall, she had to ride it clear to the college, which is ten miles away. The SKAT bus runs only three times a day, so if she rode it, she would have had to skip her high school classes.

She's determined to be independent and responsible. I could get through my day without a car, so I started loaning her the Mazda. It was easier than seeing her trying so hard. At first Trish was worried about insurance, but Kristen asked Bonnie, and she's covered on their policy whether Sterling likes it or not. She has this card in her wallet to prove it in case she gets stopped. Because she has a license and lives in his house, his company makes him cover her.

It's never as simple as some adults want it to be.

Or me either.

Wayne M. Johnston taught English, Creative Writing and Publications at La Connor High School in La Conner, Washington for nineteen years. For twenty-two years prior to that, he worked on tugboats, usually as chief engineer, towing freight barges between Canadian and American West Coast ports. In 2011 he won the *Soundings Review* First Publication Award for his essay, "Sailing." For his debut novel, *North Fork*, he drew from his experience in reading student journals to reproduce the way kids voice matters to a trusted adult.

North Fork started with a prompt Mr. Johnston presented several years ago to students in his Creative Writing class. A rough version of Natalie's entry in the sixth chapter was the response he himself produced. The story stayed with him and evolved into the novel. He would like to thank his students, colleagues, friends and family members who read the several drafts of the book and offered encouragement, with special thanks to Erin Brown whose positive response early on kept the author's belief in the book alive.

Mr. Johnston lives with his wife, Sally, on Fidalgo Island in Washington state where he is working on another book.